the city mother

To Anne —
Thank you for
sharing a wonderful
evening — Best wishes!

Maya Sinha

the city mother

a novel by
maya sinha

CHRISM
PRESS

This is a work of fiction. All characters and events portrayed in this novel are either fictitious or used fictitiously.

THE CITY MOTHER

Cover images from Shutterstock
Cover design by Rhonda Ortiz

Chrism Press, a division of WhiteFire Publishing
13607 Bedford Rd NE
Cumberland, MD 21502

ISBN:
978-1-941720-81-3 (paperback)
978-1-941720-82-0 (digital)

For RJH and PJH

1

I WAS HAVING A PLEASANT CHAT WITH MY NEW THERAPIST, JANINE, BUT when she asked about hallucinations, I clammed up. We were not going there.

"I'm not sure what you're talking about," I said. I had not washed my hair and wore maternity jeans and a gunmetal sweatshirt, its hood bunched protectively around the back of my neck like a cowl. "I tend to daydream, but nothing out of the ordinary."

"All right," she said, making a quick note. "From what you've told me about your symptoms, Cara, it sounds like you've been feeling anxious and depressed. Would you agree?"

"Yes, I guess you could say that."

"And when did these feelings begin?" She was not a medical doctor but had a counseling credential and gave the impression of a wise, practical person: short gray hair, dangly earrings, linen separates, and foot-shaped shoes. The room was decorated with framed prints of streams and rivers, a lotus floating on the surface of a pond, a water theme suggesting minds rinsed of all agitating thoughts.

"Oh, probably around the time my son was born. He's eighteen months now."

"And have these feelings increased over time, or stayed the same?"

"Um. Probably increased."

"Okay. And now you're pregnant with your second child?"

"That's right."

"And you're more tired, maybe having morning sickness?"

"Check and check."

"And how's your sleep?"

"Well, my son's not a sleeper. He sleeps with me—me and my husband. He has his own bed in our room. Plus, there's a crib, but he just naps in it. We're thinking the baby might use it. He starts out in his bed, then moves into our bed around one or two a.m. Sometimes my husband swaps beds with him, and some nights he moves to the couch. There really isn't room for three of us because Charles squirms and kicks a lot. We've tried an air mattress in the living room so one of us can get some sleep. But Charles—"

"Have you tried sleep training?"

"What, 'cry it out'? We'd like to, but we really can't. The guy who lives downstairs keeps a log—a written log, on graph paper—of all our noises. He's always complaining to the landlord about how we walk across the floor at night, or how Charles is up before dawn, crying. Or how my husband watches TV on the couch or the floor in the middle of the night, as I mentioned, after Charles moves into our bed. So, no. We can't really stick him somewhere and have him scream all night. Where would we put him?"

"So, you're not sleeping well."

"Oh, definitely not! But not because I 'can't sleep,' per se. More like I'm not *allowed* to sleep."

"I see." Another quick note, maybe in old-school shorthand, or checking a box. "And how is your relationship with Charles?"

"Normal, I'd say. He's a good baby. Active. We spend a lot of time together."

"And prior to this, you were a…" She ran a finger down the office intake form, squinting in an attempt to decipher my writing. "Copy editor, is that right? But you have not gone back to work?"

"That's right. I was a journalist for a while, and after we moved here for my husband's job, I worked as a copy editor for a trade magazine. And now I just stay home with Charles."

"And you haven't gone back to work because…?"

I took a deep breath and exhaled. This therapy session had been my husband's idea, in part because he couldn't figure out why I would not go back to work.

"Well, I didn't really enjoy my job," I said. "The bloom was kind of off the rose by that time. And it didn't pay much anyway, so it made more sense to stay home with Charles."

"I understand. Now, your depression. How would you describe—"

"Well, I actually don't think I'm depressed."

"You don't? But you said earlier—"

"It's more anxiety. I feel pretty good, it's just—"

"Okay, your anxiety. Let's focus on that. How often would you say—"

"But I don't really think that's me, either."

"Pardon?"

"I don't think these feelings are just something I dreamed up, in a vacuum. I think I'm reacting to something that's actually there."

"I'm not suggesting your anxieties are 'dreamed up' or not real, but there are certain physiological changes, hormonal fluctuations, that take place."

"Yeah, but I don't think it's hormonal. I mean, that may help me *perceive* it. There was probably some evolutionary advantage to heightened perception after birth, so that your baby didn't get dragged off by a neighboring tribe, or plucked from your arms to be sacrificed in some ritual to make the crops grow, or whatever. You had to anticipate that stuff, or your kid would be toast."

"…I'm not sure I'm following you."

"Here's the thing," I said, uncrossing my legs and leaning forward. "In medieval times, the tallest building in town was a church or cathedral. It was this beautiful, inspiring structure, but also covered with monsters and demons."

Janine adjusted her glasses. She had stopped taking notes and gazed at me with new, skeptical interest. "You mean gargoyles?"

"Right. Gargoyles. They were right there, out in the open. On the rain gutters. Over the door. Sticking their tongues out, leering at you with fangs, mooning you, up there in full view. Hand-carved and cast in stone—somebody had gone to a lot of trouble. And why? To represent that side of life! To let you know you weren't going crazy!"

"So, you're unhappy that there are no… Let me put it another way. You have these thoughts that you don't feel are being acknowledged? In modern architecture?"

"Right! Everything is so *clean*—so fun and nice and pleasant! iPad! Wi-Fi! Vente Latte! Baby Gap! And on and on. But I think maybe

I've been seeing it all wrong. When I had Charles, everything seemed different." I searched for the words to describe the problem I had with the city: how it had turned from a sophisticated place where we aspired to belong into something else altogether.

With the arrival of a baby, I felt, the city changed. Its fusion restaurants and shoe boutiques and microbreweries held no enticement for new parents sobered up by the cold shock of responsibility. Its target was a younger crowd: a throng of innocents, in thrall to simple pleasures.

Now an impression nagged at me that the city was withholding vital information about what kind of world loomed up all around us, requiring unknown tools and strategies: unnamed, unbuyable, and unsuspected. Was the city—at this vulnerable juncture of my life— emotionally abusing me, all tender promises and misdirection? Was it isolating me, wearing me down, until I lost all sense of what was real? Was I being *gaslighted*?

"The nineteenth century French poet Baudelaire," I told my therapist, "was freaked out by the city, too. He was the poet of the Paris slums. He willingly spent his whole life there, except for one ill-fated trip to Belgium—the Belgians were an incredibly rude people, he never should have gone—but he was obsessed with what an appalling, sinister place the city was."

"And so, you identify with this… French poet, is that right?" Janine jotted a longer note and frowned.

"Yes! He spent a lot of time wandering the streets like I do, with Charles in the stroller, feeling horrified and, I guess, depressed. Also, his mind was deteriorating due to syphilis. And of course the heavy drinking, the opium, and whatever else. But in one poem, he talks about how he keeps seeing the same grotesque old man all over Paris, everywhere he goes. And I get that. I really do. Only, I don't have time to write poems about it."

"Because you have a child," Janine said, glancing uneasily at my baby bump.

"That's right. And there, the resemblance ends. Baudelaire thought it was funny to order steaks 'as tender as a baby's brain.' He didn't really care for children."

Her frown intact, Janine committed this to paper. She eyed me over tortoiseshell glasses. "Have you ever considered an antidepressant?"

She began ticking off brand names I somehow already knew: a celebrity lineup of psych meds, the A-list. Then she explained the effects of selective serotonin reuptake inhibitors, considered harmless during pregnancy although there were no studies proving this, exactly. "And if you're not comfortable with that," she added, "you might consider taking up yoga. It's great for stress relief, and many women find it beneficial during pregnancy."

I could see by the clock our time was running out. Some part of me—the part that felt unseen, unheard—wanted to needle Janine a bit.

"I've tried a few different types. Ashtanga, which focuses on alignment. Bikram, which, as I'm sure you know, you do in a hundred-degree studio, all sweaty. Neither appealed to me that much. Before I got pregnant, I practiced my own version occasionally."

"Oh good!"

"I call it Smoking Yoga." Between two fingers, I waved an invisible cigarette in the air. It made me feel like a 1930s movie star, like Bette Davis of the famous eyes. "Basically, you—"

"Let me stop you right there," said Janine. She spent a long, ruminative moment looking at her notes. I waited.

"Why…?" Janine began to say, then stopped. She tried again: "What are you hoping to get out of these sessions, Cara?"

Now I was the one at a loss for words. To get my husband off my back? To keep pretending to be normal? To have, at last, someone to listen to my strange and getting-stranger thoughts? To calm down so my dark moods didn't harm my growing baby?

"I really don't know." There wasn't much Janine could do for me. There was only one thing I wanted, and that was to get out of the city.

2

FOUR YEARS AFTER I ARRIVED, IT WAS HARD TO RECALL WHY I MOVED to the city. It had something to do with a poster on my wall back home, sent by a college friend when I was still in high school: a stylized image of the city's iconic silhouette against the sky, rendered in shades of gray and dusty, dreamy pink. There were no people up so high, just geometric shapes and clouds, so in my mind the city seemed to be a place of austere beauty, a higher plane.

It had something to do with my mother, an academic at a backwater state school who claimed to want a more glamorous life for me. Since my childhood, she'd urged me to get out of town and go make something of myself.

It had a lot do with reading and the movies. I was by nature an escapist, always ready to be wherever I was not.

But the main reason I moved to the city involved my husband, Tim. And indirectly, I suppose, our future children.

I BELIEVE TIM MARRIED ME FOR MY THEORY ABOUT THE MOVIE *FARGO*. He'd been tacking toward a more conventional wife, perhaps a cheerful blonde who grew her own basil and liked to ski. I was nothing like that, but on a long car trip I explained my *Fargo* theory and it charmed him on some deep, reckless level. He threw his standards out the window and proposed to me weeks later.

My *Fargo* theory was this: The fact that police officer Marge Gunderson is pregnant is not just a comic touch—Marge waddling out to inspect corpses in the snow—but central to the film's dark vision of humanity. Every time the TV is on, the subject is birth: a primal world of sex, gore, and struggle. Meanwhile, the people of North Dakota are bland and chipper. In them, the raging infant self has been replaced, in a process like freezing, with harmless banality.

Except when it hasn't. So, there are two kinds of villains in *Fargo*: the criminals from out of town—existentially, from nowhere—and the car salesman who hires them to kidnap his wife and hold her for ransom. The salesman behaves like those around him but privately exists in a blood-red world of lies, violence, and pain. Captured by police in a motel room, he screams and writhes, regressed to infantile rage: a naked, maskless human.

In the movie's last scene, Marge is heavily pregnant and dressed in a nightgown.

"Two more months," her husband says, marking the time until another shrieking, red-faced creature arrives on the scene.

"Two more months," Marge repeats, the final words before the credits roll.

A new person is barreling into the world, exploding into white, sterile North Dakota like a force of nature. Marge's struggles with the raw material of humanity—her pained perplexity at wild, not-nice behavior—have just begun, and they're about to get a lot closer to home.

I delivered this speech with the *élan* of an A-student: a clever girl who could make up theories all day, slinging out piping hot textual analysis like a line cook in a country diner. Smiling winsomely at my boyfriend, I didn't dream it would have anything to do with me.

BACK THEN, TIM AND I BOTH WERE SMALL-TOWN NEWSPAPER REPORTERS in our twenties. I'd spent two decades reading novels, indifferent to current events. Out in the real world, where no one was going to pay me to read books, I was the City Hall reporter and barely knew where City Hall was.

I met Tim at a public meeting of the municipal water board. The night was running long, with malcontents lining up for the mic. He had a story to file and was muttering insults about each new speaker preventing him from getting back to the office to write it. "I have actual work to do," he hissed at me as I slumped in a nearby folding chair, doodling on my notepad. "But I keep getting interrupted by the stupid *news*."

"Are you Tim Nielsen from the *Star*?" Only three local reporters (including me) covered these meetings, and I figured he wasn't the one named Deb.

"Why? What do you know about him?" asked Tim.

"I read your stories all the time. I pictured you as older. They're so—"

"Dry? Pedantic? Go ahead, I can take it."

"Thorough. I call the same people as you, but you get so much more information. They tend to blow me off."

"Do you drink with them?"

"No."

"Well, that's your problem. Oh, not this one again. Wasn't she up an hour ago? Who do you write for?"

I told him.

"The weekly?" he replied. "Oh. No, it's a good paper. Seriously, you guys do some good investigative stuff. If only I had deadlines once a week! Must be nice. You're probably going home after this. What's your name?"

I told him.

"Ah. Hello, Cara. I think I've seen your stuff. You write the, the—"

There were four staff reporters at the weekly paper. We were spread thin, forced by necessity to disregard the bulk of local news. So we focused on things we liked: murder, arts, or the gay community. We each carved out a niche and burrowed away. When not covering the city or crime beats, I threw myself into reviewing films and soon became a regular at the two p.m. matinee. But I was also developing an interest in a kind of news: the human news, as I thought of it, difficult and densely-layered. City Hall's problems didn't excite me, but I was fascinated by its hapless spokesman: his wet, sad eyes and air of shiftiness, his pink shirt and too-shiny tie. It seemed to me that a subtle thread of something not-quite-ordinary ran through many ordinary events: the hyper-real. It fizzed and hummed in the silence between the question and the answer. With my pen paused above my notebook, I tried to listen to it. For it.

"—the movie reviews. Right?"

"Right. When I'm not doing this."

"They're good. You have an interesting take on things."

"Well, thanks."

"This guy again? Just kill me now. Say, what are you doing around eleven?"

"Tonight?"

"Yep. Some of us gotta work, you know. We have what's known as a newspaper coming out tomorrow."

"Well, normally I'd be hanging out with my cat at that hour. Why do you ask?"

"You have a cat? Why don't you come out for a drink with me instead? The cat will understand."

In those first moments, I saw Tim as tall, golden-haired, out of my league. He looked like the smart and slightly spoiled son of a doctor, which he was. I had been seeing a bossa nova player who wore a pork pie hat and strummed "The Girl from Ipanema" on a guitar in lieu of conversation.

"Okay. You're on."

When I recall that year, I see a backdrop of exquisite seasons: clear summer days in sundresses and sandals, walking down tree-lined streets with a cloth bag slung over one shoulder, eating an ice cream cone. One day the dress was white cotton, ankle-length, and as I passed, an old man standing in his yard remarked that I was beautiful. I smiled at him, because why not? My hair fell to my waist; my clothes were rumpled, picked up off the floor; I had twenty dollars to my name, soon to be spent on mimosas on a downtown patio.

The autumn air smelled like wood and leaves and fire, like transformation. Over huge plates of oily noodles at a Vietnamese restaurant, Tim and I gossiped about everyone we'd ever known. We shooed his roommate out of the house and watched classic films on a batik-print futon. We cooked roast lamb with fresh rosemary, played bluegrass music, swapped sections of *The New York Times*, stayed in all weekend.

Winter was hushed and magical with snow: a final, proper winter. I didn't think about leaving the snow behind. I didn't know I'd miss it.

In spring, we went on long hikes in the mountains: impossible stretches of green meadow and wildflowers. Tim cast an arc of silver line over a stream as I idled nearby, waist-deep in water so clear I could see every pebble on the bottom. The turquoise sky curved from horizon to horizon: a vast, changeable dome that contained everything. Sometimes I ventured out alone on trails miles from town, with no word to anyone about where I had gone or when I would return. My hair swung down my back; I carried a water bottle and maybe a book. When groups of strangers passed me, I nodded hello. Hours later, dusty and sweaty, I returned to my waiting car and drove home. I never worried about the risk, but had a child's unthinking trust that I was beyond the reach—the notice, even—of anything that could harm me.

FRESH OUT OF COLLEGE, I HAD LED A SHELTERED LIFE: THE CHILD OF college professors, an English major good at parsing texts and passing tests. The world seemed orderly and slightly dull: you got the grades, got the job, turned in your competent work on time, and got paid. In the off-hours from earning money, you spent it: at restaurants and bars, on clothes and travel, on escaping the narrow confines of your own life at the movies. On Monday, you went back to work and started over. And this was life: the if-then universe, a bland, industrious march of cause-and-effect. I was a nice girl and dutiful daughter. I was willing and able, as far as I knew, to do everything right.

But journalism took me out of my own world, revealed to me in startling glimpses that things were much more complicated than I realized. People were not machines; their lives did not run on straight tracks. Some lives were mysteries. In fact, a great deal about the world did not make sense, and one might even say it defied comprehension.

Looking back now, only two stories I reported seem of lasting interest. The first involved the perennial problem of the town drunk. Rather, the several local drunks who were causing public nuisances and getting jailed repeatedly. My editor sent me out to find the drunkest drunk, the biggest problem. The thinking was that, from his unique perspective, light could be shed on what to do with him.

When I asked the police who this might be, they handed me an inch-thick printout listing the tiresome infractions of just one man:

Philip Livingston. Hoping to speak to him in his usual haunt, I accompanied a police officer to a gulley under an overpass near the town square. Our shoes made crunching sounds as we climbed down the crumbling slope. The flashlight's wavering disk danced over the pebbled ground before us.

"Hello?" the officer, a woman not much older than me, called out. "Anyone here?" We were now in a deep, narrow crevice with the road some feet above our heads. Under the bridge, a few dark shapes lay strewn on the ground. We walked toward them, the flashlight leaping from one still form to another.

"Do you come down here much?" I asked.

"Once or twice a week, we like to check it out," the officer replied, advancing. "There's been a lot of fights in this area, a couple of rapes. One gentleman nearly got his eye cut out with a knife last year. I still see him around occasionally."

"Rapes? Are there women down here?"

"Typically not. Hello? Everyone doing okay tonight?" One of the mounds shifted and groaned, revealing itself to be a person in a pile of blankets. He opened his eyes briefly to look at us, then closed them and rolled over. "Then there's of course alcohol poisoning," she went on, "and ODs. I just like to make sure everyone under this bridge is alive and kicking. Phil?"

Someone yelled in a high, strangled voice: "Turn it off!"

"Anyone seen Phil tonight?" Her flashlight swept the cement walls under the overpass, scrawled with graffiti; it swept the ground, littered with broken glass, beer cans, and twisted rags. An odd sensation overtook me. The air seemed to shimmer like some weird medium resembling air. The cold was not quite real cold, the people not quite real people. Something was off. Something in this world or this dimension had gone badly wrong. Livingston wasn't there, so we left.

One week later, I learned he'd been staying at a local address. Following the directions in my car, I kept shaking my head. Could this be right? The streets in this neighborhood curved elegantly into one another, past manicured lawns and stately houses. At my stop, a garden path meandered past a fountain to a half-hidden bungalow where a tinkling wind chime hung from a beam across the porch. This was nicer than any place I'd ever lived—and this was the place.

I knocked and waited. Finally, the door creaked open. Philip Livingston, with his white-blond shock of hair and a face like a magnificent ruin, opened the door. Behind him somewhere, speakers were blasting a rapturous Italian aria that filled the house.

When I asked about the house, Livingston said a friend was letting him "crash" there for a few days. He changed the subject by offering me a Coke. Then he reclined, chain-smoking, in a low-slung chair, while I asked him a series of questions and strained to hear his answers over the music. He seemed surprised, but not particularly troubled, to learn that he'd been jailed seventeen times in the past year alone. (He had lost count, but looked over the paperwork and shrugged.) In fact, being the object of journalistic attention seemed to cheer Livingston. As the interview went on, he told his story with increasing relish, as if sitting around a campfire with a captive audience of scouts, transformed by firelight into a fearsome teller of dread tales, a shaman. A large fly buzzed near his head; he shooed it away with an expansive gesture. When it came back, he cursed and laughed, smoked and cursed. His smile was unconvincing, like a facial tic.

Back at the office, I banged out a story suggesting the town needed a rehab center. Livingston came off as quirky and sympathetic: the sort of down-on-his-luck person who could turn his life around with proper treatment. But, two days after the piece ran, Livingston's irate sister called my editor from out of state, threatening to sue if we didn't run a correction. As it turned out, Livingston was not homeless or (did I really say this?) "destitute," but the heir to a considerable fortune with several houses for the choosing. After delivering an unprintable rant about our "so-called journalism," Livingston's sister slammed down the phone.

"Cara?" my editor called across the newsroom in a thin voice. "We need to talk, in my office, now."

Informed of Livingston's vast wealth, I hung my head but was, in some way, unsurprised. Something had been off about it from the start. I'd written the story that was easy, maybe even cliché: a moving plea for a rehab facility out by the highway. But there was a truer story—hidden, but peeping through here and there—of a staggering drunk who could have been drunk in a palace, drunk in a skippered yacht, drunk among like well-heeled drunks. Instead, night after night, he chose to be drunk in a ditch with vagrants; in fact, he'd chosen to be the undisputed worst of them. There was only one reason for this, it seemed to me. The reason was he liked it.

Of course, I told myself, Livingston was mad. Still, this hidden story gave me my first glimpse into a great mystery. Like the other story that stayed with me long after my time at the paper, it made me want to stick to the verifiable facts: arrest dates, court hearings, statements of the responsible local officials. Because at the center of both stories, the thing that could not be reported squatted like a toad, cold to the touch and blind, inexplicable and uncanny.

I WASN'T REALLY CUT OUT FOR THE CRIME BEAT—I PREFERRED WRITING about movies—but occasionally there was a newsworthy local crime. Against the usual backdrop of domestic violence, illicit drug sales, and property theft, there would occur a murder of shocking brutality: the beheading of a rival drug dealer, the vicious stabbing of a roommate, the rageful shaking of a baby by her mother's boyfriend. Their corpses burned in open fields, dropped down mine shafts, stuffed into Dumpsters.

The perpetrators usually got caught; months later, there would be a plea deal or trial. Justice prevailed, more or less. But not always. The second memorable story was about a boy named Jeff. Along with his parents and sisters, he lived in a stucco ranch house with a big backyard, home to a pair of honey-colored cocker spaniels. He was seven years old, the baby of the family, and often seen riding his bike up and down the wide, flat street. When I interviewed the neighbors, one of Jeff's friends, a girl of nine, told me she didn't like to play outside anymore. Her grandmother confirmed that her pink-tasseled bike now stayed in the garage.

One Sunday afternoon, Jeff's extended family—assorted aunts and teenaged cousins, a few friends from his dad's job—had a barbeque in the backyard. The backdoor to the kitchen banged open and shut all afternoon with women carrying pitchers of margaritas, spaniels dashing in and out. Men gathered in the den to catch a few minutes of football on TV. At some point, Jeff's mother told him to take a plate of foil-wrapped corn to the grill. Though his father recalled Jeff handing the plate to him, he couldn't say when. The crowd dispersed long after dark.

At ten o'clock, a police officer got a radioed call and found Jeff's father in an alley with a flashlight, calling Jeff's name. By the following Sunday, when Jeff's disappearance was the lead story on the evening news, dozens of volunteers and a thousand flyers printed with Jeff's school photo (showing a dark-haired boy with bangs and a shy grin) had turned up nothing. Where had he gone? With whom, and why? Jeff's mother was hysterical, volubly and in print. She built a shrine to Jeff that filled the living room and brought in a psychic from out of state. They searched the landfill. They dragged the lake. Crime Stoppers offered a reward for information, jamming the lines with useless leads and tips.

Time passed.

Writing these stories, I felt as nonplussed as Marge Gunderson in *Fargo*, asking a serial killer in her police car as they traverse a frozen landscape: "And for what?" Wordless, he gazes out the window at a passing statue of Paul Bunyan gripping an axe.

"And here you are," she concludes sadly. "And it's a beautiful day."

There was plenty of suffering in the natural world, described by Tennyson as "red in tooth and claw." An antelope dragged down by a lion was not having a good time. But it was not gratuitous suffering. It didn't last terribly long, it was nothing personal against the antelope, and it made perfect sense. The lion had to eat. Only humans inflicted pointless suffering, requiring new and complex terms: cruelty, depravity, murder.

Marge didn't understand it, either: What in the world was wrong with people?

Seven months pregnant, she stoically faced the future.

"Holy cow," Tim said one Saturday morning. "I got it."

He was sitting at the desk next to his bed, a slice of cold pizza in his hand, staring at a computer that rose like a temple from a jungle of books, Dr. Pepper cans, cigarette packs, and fishing tackle.

"What? Let me see." I put down my coffee cup and got out of bed to stand behind him. On the screen was an e-mail from an editor at a well-known city newspaper offering Tim a job. The start date was one month out.

"Oh my gosh."

"Honey. I got it!"

"You got it! I can't believe it. Of course, you deserve it—"

Here Tim swept me into his arms for a kiss.

"Of course, you deserve it," I repeated afterward. "Are you going to…?"

"Take it? Absolutely. I'll have to tell Mike right away. A month isn't that long. I need to find a place."

I said nothing as he Googled, talking excitedly. Several minutes in, he glanced back at me. "Cara? What's the matter?"

"Well, I'm happy for you. It's great for your career. I'm just sad when I think about… I mean, you'll be moving away. And I'll be here."

Tim's hands paused on the keyboard. He turned to face me fully. His brow furrowed as if someone had just assigned him a difficult math problem. After a long moment, he said, "That's unacceptable."

"It is?"

Three weeks before, we had been driving along the river. Out the passenger window, a timeless landscape of water, rocks, trees, and sky filled my view, a film-worthy panorama showcasing the majesty of nature. Acoustic guitar was playing on the radio, and I had an open beer bottle between my knees.

"That's my theory about *Fargo*. What do you think?"

"I think you're something else," said Tim. "The way you see things. I never would have come up with that."

"That's why they pay me the big bucks," I retorted, an old joke. All reporters were low-paid or, as we liked to think, undervalued.

"I've never met anyone like you. You're different from other girls."

The trees were turning gold. Our long and glorious summer was almost at an end.

"I always have been," I said.

WE HAD A SMALL CEREMONY IN A GROVE OF TREES. ASIDE FROM A handful of work friends, there was only my mother, Tim, and me. Tim's father was unable to fly out on short notice, as he had booked a trip to the Bahamas with his second wife and their kids. Tim's mother sent her best wishes and a check. She couldn't make it because her back was acting up.

The previous night, we'd written our own vows. Now we recited these in sandals to the strains of a violin, in a ritual performed by a middle-aged woman ordained by some tongue-in-cheek Internet church. Draped in velveteen, she resembled a wizened tree sprite who had popped out of the forest for this purpose and would soon disappear—as indeed she did—magically and forever.

Afterward, my mother embraced Tim. "I've heard so much about you," she said in her warmest voice.

Had she? I tried to recall what I had told my mother, Claudia, about him. It seemed to amount to the fact that he was not the bossa nova player and had a real job. Now having gotten even more real, his job was taking us away, away.

In a pewter-colored suit and Balinese jewelry, Claudia looked elegant, composed. She did not seem troubled by the fact that I was moving out of state with my new, sandal-wearing husband and would not be a three-hour drive from home. After all, I was following the plan she had laid out: leaving this podunk state behind, abandoning small towns where only losers stayed. Like other faculty kids whose parents were stranded here for work, I was embarking on my own glorious liftoff: up and out.

In fact, Claudia and I didn't see each other very often. I was her second (and only surviving) child, and our relationship seemed cool compared to other mothers and daughters. We didn't get pedicures together, we didn't bake. A tenured professor, she spent a lot of time in her home office, the radio tuned to classical music and news. Growing up, if I needed anything, I knew to knock.

Still, it felt strange to be moving thousands of miles away. The last time I'd moved out of state, for college, it hadn't gone well. Far from home, I had become disoriented, unstable.

"You'll visit soon?" I asked.

"Of course! As soon as the semester's over, I'd love to come. You know how things are in the fall."

Two days later, Tim maneuvered our packed U-Haul into the street. The cat sat, stunned, in a carrier on my lap. Planning to drive through the night, we wended through the town at dusk, its familiar buildings and parks bathed in a golden light. Great pink clouds unfurled over the highway, a dark ribbon that unspooled toward the horizon. I realized that I would probably never live here again. Even if I came back, something was ending, had already ended.

Anyway, the boy was never found.

3

THERE IS A DESK IN HERE. WRITING GIVES ME SOMETHING TO FILL THE empty hours—unbelievable, that I should suddenly have so much free time. Plucked from my real life, I can finally hear myself think.

Today marks three days in the Mildred W. Ehrlinger Psychiatric Hospital, an imposing brick structure ten miles or so outside the city. Built a century ago, it was named for a wealthy industrialist's wife, committed here after she insisted a whistling teapot was speaking to her— shrieking to her of her imminent doom—in code. That's what I imagine, anyway, from the large portrait of a silver-haired dowager in the main hall. There is something shifty in her expression, some unspeakable secret withheld, waiting for somebody to finally notice and ask the right question. Or maybe she was just an ordinary woman, and it's my own imagination running wild.

I'm in a small room with a narrow bed, a slab jutting out from the wall that functions as a desk or table, and a chair. For the past two nights, I've slept fitfully under thin blankets, on a pillow encased in noisy plastic. I'm still wearing the clothes I came in: a Willie Nelson T-shirt, a baggy cardigan, jeans, and the slipper-like clogs I wear around the house. Most people here are in street clothes, though I've noticed that their shoelaces have been removed. Also, their belts. A few of them pad around in socks, as if hoping—perhaps *believing*—this is all a big slumber party and, any minute now, we'll start French braiding each other's hair.

I keep to myself as much as possible, though nurses, social workers, and fresh-faced staffers with clipboards are always popping by my room. I've gone from being the one who watches the kids to the one being checked *on*, and I recognize their casual, sharp-eyed manner as they scan for anything amiss.

But I'm just sitting here scribbling most of the time. Yesterday morning, I asked for a pen and paper, and the young man with the clipboard gave me a wary look. His job requires him to take nothing at face value, to assume every request is some kind of dangerous ruse.

"Look, I'm a journalist," I said in my most professional voice, wishing I was not wearing a shirt with a guitar and a bald eagle on it. "I would just like to take some notes during my stay. To help me organize my thoughts and…process things."

"I'll ask the doctor," he said, studying the form on his clipboard for any special note, like no pens.

That afternoon, a different orderly came by and placed a legal pad and hollow plastic ballpoint on my desk. After giving me a pointed look—*don't make me regret this*—she left.

From a high corner, a small camera keeps its glassy eye on me, feeding real-time video into a row of monitors somewhere on the floor. It's not much of a movie, I imagine, shot in grainy black-and-white with low production values and a sluggish, silent cast of one. As a narrative, it lacks backstory, character development, and any semblance of a plot. *A dark-haired woman sits on her bed. She stands and gazes out the window. She tries to take a nap and fails. Finally, she picks up a pen and starts to write.*

This is the film the nurses want to see, mirrored in dozens of small rooms throughout the day. Like a mother glancing at the baby monitor, reassured by the rhythmic rise and fall of the bundle under the covers, theirs is an aesthetic of normalcy, of no-news-is-good-news. The continuation of the hard-earned ordinary is the goal.

That is all very well. But I myself have bigger fish to fry.

Outside my window, three orange butterflies circle and re-circle a bit of green. Every day, they reappear in the same spot and hover there, to no apparent purpose. It seems significant: always three, only three. Four with one missing.

I am trying to collect my thoughts, to recall how all this happened, so I am writing it down from the beginning. The main thing now is to remain calm, to *present* as calm. I need to get out of here and get back to the children.

And the other thing.

4

As I recall, I was delighted at the first sight of my prison.

"It's incredible," I said, standing before a row of picture windows from which a sunlit lake could be seen in the near distance. "We have to live here."

"It's over budget," said Tim. "But it's going to be hard to turn down."

"We're just lucky this one's available. I was starting to get worried. Everything else was just—"

"Well?" The property management woman emerged from the galley kitchen, painted a buttery yellow, smiling. "What do you two think?"

Tim said, "It's so close to downtown, I can bike to work. What was the down payment, again? It shouldn't be a problem."

Built on a lakeside slope during the city's housing boom, our building blended Art Deco and Spanish styles: a deep red structure with accents in creamy white. Bas-relief metal doors opened into a high foyer with espresso-colored tiles and a coffered ceiling: sunken gold squares stamped with a floral pattern four stories up. A tiled staircase with a cast-iron banister led up to the mezzanine. To the left was an elevator with a metal grille and a knobby black button for each numbered floor above the lobby, which was simply *L*. On the fourth and highest floor, a burgundy carpet with a gold and purple pattern ran the length of the hall, ending at our door: 3C.

The apartment consisted of a bedroom, bathroom, galley kitchen, dining room, and a long, narrow living room that ended in a row of silver-latched windows. A closet-sized nook contained a built-in desk and shelves, perfect for Tim. We brought in our now-shared furniture, culled from two bachelor apartments: an ancient tan leather couch, worn white in places; a high-backed chair and a low-slung modern chair; a multi-colored Persian rug, a table, a bed. We hung framed prints, stacked our wedding dishes in the yellow cupboards, bought six large pots, and planted red geraniums under the windows.

In those early weeks, I felt swept up in an exhilarating new life. I was no longer a nerdy loner hanging around small-town meetings, but a wife and city dweller, an urban sophisticate with a man on my arm. I had not planned any of this, but scudded along like a twig in a stream, and this was where the current swept me: into the city of my sophomore daydreams, the place I'd always hoped I would visit when I got my braces off. Holding Tim's hand as we strolled the downtown streets, I could hardly believe I lived here, deep in a dense matrix of tall buildings and crowds that collectively emitted a low, unceasing roar.

"I'm such a country mouse," I murmured, startled by the abrupt bleat of a horn as a taxi swerved to avoid a blue-haired bike messenger outside a sex shop.

Tim slung his right arm around my shoulders and gave an affectionate squeeze. "Not anymore."

I DIDN'T KNOW MUCH ABOUT OUR NEIGHBORS IN THE BUILDING. I saw them in passing and tried and failed to remember their names. There was the Old Woman, the Aesthete, the Mother and Middle-Aged Daughter, the Angry Ballerina, the Missionaries—a pious, quiet family of four—and the Man Downstairs. Sometimes we'd see the Aesthete, a bald, pink-cheeked man of about forty, collecting his mail from the metal boxes by the lobby elevator.

"Just more junk!" he would cheerfully announce. "Bills, advertising flyers, the Yale alumni magazine, of course! They're always wanting me to donate. My name is Brighton, by the way."

We introduced ourselves and realized he lived across the hall. He had a job in investment banking and played the cello as a musician-for-hire. He'd worked on film scores and at society weddings. In his spare time, he attended lectures on calligraphy, the Japanese tea ceremony, and olive oil. He was a fascinating person, but every conversation, however brief, included an incongruous mention of college:

"You're working for the city paper? That's great. I worked on the *Yale Daily News* one year and loved it. Good for you!"

"Dogs? I think it's on a case-by-case basis. Are you thinking about a dog? My flatmate senior year at Yale had a dog, a Chow, and I swore to myself, never again!"

Lying in bed, Tim and I dreamed up new scenarios:

"A buddy of mine's coming out from Connecticut," Tim would say casually. "Ever been there?"

"I notice this city has several junior colleges," I'd pipe up. "That's great for some people, but personally, I'm glad I attended a four-year college. What about you, Brighton?"

"Out in Texas," quipped Tim, "they have this word: *Y'all*. It means you all. Y'all come back now! It's an odd word, y'all. YAY-AWWWWWWL."

We giggled like kids and dove under the covers.

TIM THREW HIMSELF INTO HIS NEW JOB. HE WENT IN EARLY AND CAME home late, eager to talk about his day: a blend of office politics and developing news.

Newspaper openings were hard to come by, so I applied broadly. Within a month, I had a copyediting job at a trade journal. Its offices were on a wide, blustery street—a known wind tunnel—where I emerged from the subway to debris blowing hither and thither. Plastic bags pressed against my legs, empty cans rolled across my path. People clutched at their coats and purses, staggering against the wind. The smell was slightly putrid, trash dancing merrily in mid-air. My loose hair blowing in my face, tweed skirt flapping around my knees, I hobbled down the crosswalk, dodging errant cars, in too-tight pointy shoes.

"Smile!" some man would yell occasionally—always a different guy, sometimes behind the wheel of a delivery truck and, other times, splayed in a puddle of vomit beside a Dumpster—as if the entire male sex found me off-putting.

Once inside the building where I worked, the air was canned and still. I'd ride the elevator to the seventh floor in silence.

"Good morning."

"Good morning."

"Morning."

"Morning."

My boss was a pleasant young man named Ben whose family owned this obscure publication, among others. Married with twin three-year-old girls, Ben seemed domesticated, earnest, tired. His management style was to smile wearily, run a hand through his hair, and say, "Sure. Great. Thanks!"

Compared to reporting, copy editing was technical and dry. The most interesting part of the day was lunch, which I often spent with a woman my age named Gemma who had been on the editorial staff six months. She was a pale, freckled blonde and held the mild fascination of being my opposite physical type. With long, dark hair and faint hereditary undereye shadows, I looked like the Victorian poet Christina Rossetti after a three-day bender.

Gemma had already scoped out the neighborhood and led me through a maze of unpromising streets to one that was simply adorable: a secret alley of delicacies and delights. A row of old brick buildings had been converted into hemp boutiques, galleries of cartoon art, artisanal tea bars, vegan shoe stores. We ate salads in airy cafés with a French-industrial vibe. We lunched on noodles and raw fish served in lipstick-red lacquer boxes. We mm'd and ahh'd over fried chicken sandwiches served with sweet mint tea in Mason jars. Our work was boring, but Gemma and I made a point to lunch like queens.

Gradually, the city was changing Tim and me. We expected more out of our weekends; we had more interests, if you could call them that. Our off-hours were now filled with open mic nights, readings, live jazz. Tim joined a downtown gym and started playing racquetball at lunch. We tried newly invented drinks in retro pinball bars and tiki lounges. In the grocery store, we found ourselves voicing strong opinions about cheeses. On Saturdays, we trekked under the freeway to the farmer's market, held in a large parking lot by the lake, where we spent hours evaluating vegetables and drinking beer at plastic tables to the strains of a mandolin band. Tim talked about trying CrossFit. I decided all my old clothes were drab. We stood in line for forty-five minutes to eat breakfast and play board games with strangers.

On the phone, Claudia seemed proud of me as I described our outings. She was a widow, and my only sibling, a boy named David, had died in infancy, so there was not much family gossip. As a small-town reporter who'd spent most of her free time with the cat, I'd sometimes sensed my calls bored Claudia; the city gave us new material to discuss. She came out once or twice a year, and Tim and I flew home for Christmas. Tim's mother visited once, hobbling out of a Boeing 747 dressed in head-to-toe leopard print. After two hours of sharing her opinions on various matters, she declared to me, with Tim in earshot, "You're too good for him!"

The months passed quickly. Tim quit smoking and bought a high-end lime-green bike. He hung it on the wall.

On any given Friday night or Sunday afternoon, Tim and I would look up the local showtimes and go to the movies. The city's old Art Deco theaters made us feel like part of history, enacting a timeless ritual. The uniformed man in the box office handed us our tickets and we walked down a sloped red carpet into a dark hall, where a series of closed doors presented themselves for the choosing. A distinctive smell of buttered popcorn, dusty velvet, brass polish, and the perfume-and-dirty sneaker odors of a crowd permeated the air. In a year or two, everyone would be staring down at smartphones, but when we first lived in the city, Tim and I would sit side by side, people-watching before the theater lights dimmed, entertained by nothing more than our own silly banter.

We were like children in those days, and the city a playground to explore. We filled the fridge with takeout cartons and let the plants die, the furniture gather dust. To keep ourselves amused on weeknights, we put a TV in the bedroom and binge-watched critically acclaimed dramas, gratified by our own good taste, an open pizza box between us.

We seemed so well-suited, two people enjoying a magical rapport. We were alive, basking together in the screen's blue glow, the generations that produced us fallen away into oblivion. We had escaped our lonely homes, abandoned our complicated pasts—Tim had been sent to boarding school at twelve as his family disintegrated—and set out for the promised land of great jobs, amazing views, and pan-ethnic cuisine. It was all going to work out for us, the plucky young heroes, bravely pressing forward hand-in-hand like children in a fairy tale.

Sometimes, I'd wake up in the middle of the night just to reassure myself that Tim was there, lightly snoring beside me. I'd study his sleeping face, the inscrutable mask of my own destiny.

OF COURSE, ONCE IN A WHILE, OUR RAPPORT BROKE DOWN.

"I've heard good things about the new Cambodian restaurant," Tim remarked one day.

"Oh?" I said.

"We should try it this weekend."

"Mm."

"You don't sound too excited."

"Well, it just reminds me of…Cambodia."

"It's supposed to! It's said to be very authentic."

"No, I mean the Khmer Rouge. When I hear *Cambodia*, I immediately think of rows of skulls. Mass graves. That sort of thing."

"The Khmer Rouge?" Tim lowered his book and peered over it. "That was, like, fifty years ago. The owners are probably refugees, or the children of refugees."

"I know, I know. And I want to support them! The thing is, though, when I read about the Khmer Rouge in college, it was literally the worst thing I'd ever heard. Worse than the Nazis in a way, because they turned on their own people, their own family members. People were killed for crazy reasons—for picking fruit, for wearing glasses. They forced everyone out of their homes, they cut the telephone lines, they banned *forks*. They murdered all the teachers and monks. People were hauled away and shot for nothing. Millions starved. It just—"

"But it's a *restaurant*. You sound phobic. You're being a Cambodiaphobe."

"I'm not a phobe! It's not an irrational fear of anyone. I don't think a Cambodian's going to run out of the kitchen and stab me with a knife. It's just so horrifying, what happened in that country."

"All these people did," said Tim, "was move here and open a business—a Zagat-*rated* business. They're not the freaking Khmer

Rouge. I can't believe you're blaming Cambodian-Americans for something that happened decades ago in another hemisphere."

"I'm not blaming them! I'm sure they're no different from anybody else. It's just a reminder of how gruesome humans can be, *as symbolized by* Cambodia in the late twentieth century."

"Whatever."

WHAT WAS I WORKING FOR?

Two years into my downtown job, I could not answer that question. Tim was getting challenging assignments and his byline in the paper; he loved his work. For me, weekdays were spent shuffling through the soporific routines of office life. I joked with Ben, I lunched with Gemma, the workplace buzzed with its gentle, seat-bound demands, its abstract and mild sense of urgency disseminated through "deadlines" and "goals." It was a perfectly fine job, as jobs went. But was it a *reason* to work? No.

Growing up, I watched as Claudia spent countless hours poring over work. She took it seriously: parked at her desk late into the night, her home office a refuge from whatever tasks or interactions lurked outside it. Before he died in my late childhood, my father and I watched TV over fast food while she reworked her syllabi or graded papers.

Now I was starting to discover my own attitude toward work, and it was not the sense that I had finally found my life's mission. Everything I did there could be done by someone else just as well, so that my endgame at the office would not be glory or distinction but one day vanishing without a trace and being promptly replaced. Claudia seemed pleased that I was an office worker in the city, perhaps imagining a glamorous life she herself would have wanted. But I was not Claudia, and trudging to work five days a week in a pencil skirt to mark up texts was beginning to feel like a waste of my time.

I began to wonder whether we could live on Tim's salary alone. It would be tight. There would be less take-out sushi, fewer wine flights. I'd have to keep wearing the shoes I had. We could keep the apartment, barely. We could still go to the farmer's market, the park.

Maybe I was just lazy, but I was also feeling restless, underused. Under the high whine of the subway, under the office chat about last night's TV show, under the pleasantries of commerce as I swiped my card through the machine, a thought began to blossom that there was important work to do—specifically, for *me* to do—and this job was not it. I had not yet willed the real job into being.

What job was that? I had the merest filament of an idea, just a hunch. Throughout high school and college, I never thought of myself as maternal, but as a reader who valued peace and quiet. Wiping noses and changing diapers didn't sound like my kind of thing.

One day, however, when I was working as a newspaper reporter, the photographer's sister showed up at our office, family in tow. They were visiting from out of state, and the whole editorial staff took them to lunch. It must have been a slow news day. The hostess seated us all at a big round table, and I ended up next to the sister's children: a boy and girl, maybe eight and six. I don't remember who was on my other side, but to my surprise, the kids and I hit it off. We chatted happily for an hour, oblivious to whatever the grown-ups were saying. I had never met such delightful children. They were funny and curious and full of joy. In fact, I had spent almost no time around children since being a child myself. Was it possible there were more like this?

As they drove away with their parents, I felt a pang waving good-bye: back to the grown-up world, which now felt comparatively dreary. Some wild element was missing, some sense of playfulness or general hilarity. The grown-ups smiled less, joked less, and were less interested in what you had to say. We were all somehow less attentive to reality itself.

All this had been in the back of my mind when I married Tim. Now I was a healthy young wife, and it seemed like the time to act. Didn't someone once say fortune favors the bold?

That's how I came to utter my life's six most fateful words. We were shucking oysters at a picnic table, wearing old T-shirts, shorts, and flip-flops, when I looked up at my husband mid-shuck and said, "I want to have a baby."

5

I AM NOT A PHYSICALLY BRAVE PERSON—QUITE THE OPPOSITE. HEIGHTS scare me. Driving on the freeway makes me nervous. If a fire alarm goes off, I assume it is probably not a drill and death is imminent. I sit on towels on the beach, as the ocean could devour me at any point. Large dogs seem unpredictable; I give them a wide berth. One time, Tim tried to take me mountain biking and I started crying.

But when the nurses swiftly draped a white curtain across my chest so I would not see when the doctor cut me open, I didn't say a word. I knew I had to keep it together; this was now my paramount task. The fetal monitor couldn't find a heartbeat, and nobody knew why, and they needed to get the baby out. The doctor and I were co-pilots and we had to land this plane right away. White-faced, Tim sat at my shoulder and held my hand, but Tim was a nobody, a steward. Tim was serving drinks as the cabin lurched through the sky. I had to land the plane. I *was* the plane. My sheet-draped lower body was the plane.

Up in the cockpit, my brain worked the controls with studied calm. "C, one. H, two. A, three," I said. The operating theater was bright white. Beyond the curtain, a doctor worked quietly while two nurses hovered. I could not stand the sight of blood, and this curtain was now my favorite object on earth. "R, four. I'm counting the letters of his—L, five—of his name," I said to Tim.

"It's going to be okay," he whispered hoarsely.

"E, six. S, seven. His first name has seven letters!" I announced as if solving a puzzle. Tim looked stunned. I continued on my fingers: "J, one. O, two."

The baby's first name had seven letters. He was going to be just fine, because his lucky name was waiting for him. It was important not to distract the doctor, so I kept my voice low. His middle name had six letters. His last name also lucky seven. Seven six seven. Seven hundred and sixty-seven. Twenty letters.

I did not look down at the curtain, where God knows what was going on, but up into the big white light. "C, one. A, two. R, three," I began. My whole name had so many letters, I lost count. The numbers were helping me not to think, but I couldn't add. It was too much. It didn't matter. The baby's name had seven letters. I kept going.

"T, one. I, two. M—"

A high, ragged cry interrupted me.

"*Is he okay?*"

"The baby's fine," the doctor answered. Tears wet my face. At that moment, I loved all doctors; all of them were heroes. We had landed the plane, and everybody was safe on the ground. Someone held the red, wrinkled baby up near my face, and Tim took a photo. The nurses whisked him off, and Tim stepped away while the doctor sewed me up.

In this surreal scene, the anesthesiologist, Dr. Rodd—a tall, shaggy man who was hands-down my favorite person in the world, including Tim and the baby, because he had rigged it so I didn't feel it when they *cut me open*—came up beside me, took my hand, and shook it.

His words have stayed with me always: "You were a soldier."

CHARLES JOSEPH NIELSEN WAS NOW A PERSON, A GOING CONCERN. They wrote his name on the whiteboard in my recovery room, shocking me with his reality. A human being had entered history through the unlikely conduit of my own body, which had never seemed good for much but putting food into and hanging clothes on. Tim, too, had somehow been involved. Between the two of us, we could not keep a plant alive—the geraniums had long since withered—yet here we were.

The night nurse ripped a blood pressure cuff off my arm and, at the sound of Velcro separating, the baby startled, his limbs shaking. For the first time in his six-hour life, he began to cry with fear.

Like people stoned or dumbstruck, Tim and I laughed.

"Oh no! He doesn't like Velcro!"

"The Velcro's scaring him!"

"Bad Velcro!"

The nurse left, chuckling. I bounced him up and down, and he went back to sleep. "Poor Charles," I said softly.

TIM SPENT THAT FIRST NIGHT IN A CHAIR, THE BABY IN A LUCITE bassinet between us. Catheterized and on strong painkillers, I had entered a sort of twilight state. At points throughout the night, someone would gently wake me and hand him to me.

In the spaceship light of a bedside lamp, I nursed him. He was a baby, that was all: a furled, pink, symmetrical baby. But for his perfectly round head—airlifted rather than pushed through a tunnel—he had no distinguishing features. Yet, he was *my* baby, a special baby. He was officially the center of my life.

Well, we would get to know each other. There seemed no particular rush. I now knew he didn't like Velcro. Also, he was not blind or physically deformed. This seemed like a promising start to our relationship. Had I had any sleep? What time was it?

It didn't matter. The baby slept in my arms, Tim on the chair. The whole experience might have lasted three hours or three minutes. Out of my altered mind, a series of children's songs unspooled into the air, half-remembered and half-imagined, rhyming, warbling, oddly syncopated, telling the baby about cows and moons and apples and little lambs and grocery stores and computers and airplanes and jokes and Daddy and me and him and his whole family.

THE APARTMENT HAD BEEN MADE READY, OUTFITTED IN A LONG SPASM of acquisition. One day I'd woken up and perceived with lightning clarity that our living space was unsuitable for babies. Tim's office nook, for example, was crammed with papers, books, and assorted cast-off junk, and this was an eyesore, directly in the line of sight of my new rocking chair. Our linen cupboard was a mess; we needed room for more blankets. The kitchen windowsill, where a line of corks and beer bottle caps glinted in the sun, was idiotic; we needed succulents or herbs, something from nature, as one might find in an actual *kitchen*.

The bedroom dresser had to be emptied, repainted powder blue, and filled with all new things. It had to be topped with a changing pad, and the changing pad needed its own cover. We needed a diaper pail or a Diaper Genie; reports were mixed. We needed a wipe warmer. I knew some people didn't have one, but I could not handle it unless we did. A black-and-white mobile featuring geometric shapes should dangle from the ceiling, where there now appeared to be a—yikes, *spider's nest?* We needed rattles; we needed bibs. We needed a series of small, indestructible books that could be chewed on and pooped on and still convey the necessary information. Did we need a mural of giraffes, a giant "C" over the changing table? No, that was vulgar, that was trite. We were intellectuals!

Claudia dispatched herself to the city, and the two of us solemnly folded and stacked onesies. I was now about eight months pregnant and quite large. "Has anyone done the math on this?" I kept saying, glancing down meaningfully at my lower half. "Is this even physically possible?" Tim and my mother both looked at the ground and said nothing. No one, apparently, had done the math.

The Swedish crib arrived in pieces. Tim sat on the floor for two hours, fiddling with caramel-brown arcs of wood, dowels, and slats. It would start as an oval bassinet and then be reconfigured as full-size crib, and then a larger crib, and then a toddler bed-slash-prison that could not be breached by a two-year-old child. This was all Tim's problem, not mine. I sat in the rocking chair, fanning myself and drinking a glass of juice. Was I going to start crying? No, he would get it done. We would have a lovely oval bassinet. I trusted him…

At work, I begged off a baby shower, but people gave me presents anyway: little stuffed elephants, diminutive sailor suits, boxes of tiny socks. I was surprised and touched by this display and its evident sincerity. I had been just another office drone, surrounded by coworkers also waiting for the weekend or vacation; yet people I barely knew kept popping into my cubicle to give me cards and gift certificates, smiling at me like I was suddenly important. I felt like an astronaut departing for the mysteries of deep space. These were my last days in Fort Lauderdale, my last days on the ground.

"Thank you," I said, over and over. "That's so nice of you. Thanks so much."

"I can't wait to see him," Gemma said. "You have to call me as soon as he's here!"

"I know you probably won't come back," said Ben, half-sitting on the edge of my desk. I had just left a meeting early because my feet were going numb. He waved it off: No problem. Normal. "But you always can if you want. Don't be a stranger."

I QUEENED IT OUT OF THE HOSPITAL IN A WHEELCHAIR, THE BABY IN MY arms. The nurse—whom I had known two days and seemed to "get" me better and show more fine-grained concern for my well-being than my own family—wheeled us down the hall and through a large glass door whose panels parted at our approach. We emerged onto a sidewalk facing the parking lot. Outside, the day was gray and wet. Tim pulled up, got out of the car, and began fiddling with the car seat.

The nurse and I waited. She seemed to know on some level that I was being pushed out of an open boat into the wide, cold sea. This understanding passed between us as a brisk wind ruffled my wraps. I was hormonal, drugged, post-surgical. The wintry city, viewed objectively, was no place for a baby. There were cars everywhere, bad weather, a general surliness, a sense of clotted dreams.

"All ready?" Tim called out.

"Ready!" I said.

Tim took the baby and, slowly, I stood up from the wheelchair and sat down in the car.

"CHARLES, WE'RE HOME!"

In truth, nothing in my life had made me happier than that baby. Despite the scars and discomfort, the great waves of teary exhaustion, the pills and more pills to cope with the first pills' nasty side effects, I could hardly believe the universe had handed me this infant, whose role in life was simply to hang out with me in my own bedroom.

There was nothing better for either of us to be doing; we had no place to be. Here he was in his yellow blanket, and here I was in my old nightgown, ideally attired. It was the world's best date, the most complete and perfect date. Togetherness.

We soon fell into a routine: We took baths, ate, and slept together. We slept in bed, in chairs, and on the couch. We slept at all hours of day and night. Sometimes Charles slept on my chest and sometimes on a pillow on my lap. One time I woke to find him sleeping on my head; he seemed fine, so I sensibly went back to sleep. Sleeping with Charles was like sleeping with a part of my own body, but also with a friend, a person who liked me as I was: usually asleep. There was no judgment, no social protocol, no words at all. Never in my life had I met anyone who simply wanted to sleep with me, all the time, wherever we happened to find ourselves. Occasionally, he slept with Tim, but I knew he'd soon come back to me. Within minutes of reconnecting, our breaths and heartbeats were in sync. My skin communicated comfort to his skin. He almost never cried. Why would he?

Looking back now, those weeks of sleeping all the time seem like a dream. But there are photographs to prove it: Charles and me asleep, together, dreaming.

When Charles was ten days old, Gemma came by for lunch. We thought we'd take him to a nearby restaurant, set his carrier on the table, and catch up. For the occasion, I had gotten dressed.

Turning the key to lock up the apartment, I looked down and saw that the lower half of my dress was covered in blood. I turned to Gemma, cooing at Charles in his blue carrier behind me. As soon as she saw me, she gasped.

"What happened? Are you okay?"

"I didn't even feel it," I said. "I don't know what's going on."

"You should sit down."

"My phone is in my purse," I said. "Can you call Tim?"

I went back inside and gingerly sat down on the bed. Words sprang to mind—*hemorrhage, rupture*—that sounded like serious words. Outside the bedroom, Gemma spoke in an urgent voice to Tim. The day was turning odd, unreal. She popped her head into the room and said, "He's on his way."

So much for lunch. Time seemed to slow. In the living room, Gemma rocked the baby; I could hear her voice. It seemed likely I was experiencing a *hemorrhage*, in which case I should probably sit still.

One would not want anything to *rupture*. It seemed remotely possible to bleed to death before Tim made it home.

On the nightstand were medicine bottles, a box of Kleenex, a half-empty baby bottle, and a notebook and pen. The notebook contained a pill log, tracking the times I took my painkillers. Now as I sat there, a dissociative clarity descended, a bracing sense of agency and purpose: I could make a list of things to pack for the hospital, in case I lived. *Toothbrush*, I wrote. *Underwear. Two pairs of socks.* I needed my *pills* and *pill log.* I needed some kind of snack—*pretzels*?

Trickier was the list of what Charles required in my absence. How long would I be gone? Who would take care of him? The pen hovered over the paper, waiting. Nothing came to mind.

Tim arrived to collect me for the emergency room. I didn't want to change my clothes or move at all. So, we arrived that way: me in my blood-soaked dress, Tim walking me to triage. We left Gemma holding the baby, looking like someone who had been handed a loaded gun.

A heavily tattooed male phlebotomist took my blood, failing the first few tries but finally hitting a vein. Pregnancy had involved so many bodily intrusions by so many strangers that by this time I knew my role: passive, accommodating lump. No one was interested in me as a person; they cared only about my red cell count, my centimeters of dilation, my mucous. There was no point chit-chatting with people like this; one merely waited for them to be done. I passed the time by exchanging bleak jokes with Tim.

Two hours later, a doctor came by to report that this was just one of those things that happens. Two weeks after a cesarean section, the uterus sometimes wanted to "get rid of a lot of blood." It was not a hemorrhage or rupture. It was just a bucket of extra blood that had to go somewhere, but not to worry. Now that it was done, I would probably be fine.

Tim drove me home, where, still in bloody clothes, I took the baby and curled up with him. Per my wish, everyone else went away.

AFTER THIS UNSETTLING EPISODE, I WAS AFRAID TO BE ALONE WITH Charles. I begged Tim to skip going to the gym, to be back from the grocery store in fifteen minutes. Few things seemed worth leaving us alone in the apartment, as I had zero experience caring for a baby. What if he suddenly stopped breathing? What if I went to use the bathroom and he hurt himself somehow? We were airborne without a net, except for Tim.

But after a brief paid leave, Tim was back at work. He had been getting restless at home and didn't mind leaving the baby with me. Charles felt like a physical extension of my person; being apart from him for an entire workday was unthinkable. Though I missed Tim, it was good he could go to work. Somebody had to.

So Charles and I were home alone all the time. I tried to relax into it, enjoy it. My pain medication was tapering down, but I still felt mildly buzzy: making up songs, having odd, animated conversations with the baby. Music was playing all the time: African lullabies; Celtic instrumentals; long, searching, improvised duets of sitar and steel guitar, so that the apartment seemed to thrum with its own pulse, keeping time with some universal human rhythm.

One evening, I rocked with Charles in our chair, gazing out the six windows of the living room to a grandiose sunset filled with masses of sherbet-colored clouds. The light in the room seemed finely particulate, like gold dust. Charles dozed on a pillow with room for my hands, palms-down, on either side. The rocking chair creaked in time with the music on the stereo.

Out of nowhere, a stealth wave of feeling crashed over me. The chair stopped rocking. Tears sprang to my eyes. I put my hands over my face, suddenly wet with tears and snot, and wept into them. I cried for the enormity of my task, for my own frailty. I cried because it was impossible. I didn't know how to do it. I cried for everything the world would hurl at Charles: every playground taunt, every heartbreak, every dreaded phone call to report the tests had come back positive. I cried because there was no one to hear my crying.

The music moved on as I hid my drenched face and sobbed.

6

THE PROBLEM STARTED WHEN I BEGAN HURRYING PAST THE STAIRS.
Before we had the baby, Tim and I typically took the stairs. The building's stairwell was only two doors down from our apartment and preferable to waiting on the elevator. Like the hallway, the stairs were carpeted in an Art Deco pattern of red, purple, and gold. A spindly, waist-high rail stood between the hall and the stairwell; gaudy stairs spiraled down to the foyer where espresso-colored tiles gleamed in waiting. The old, ornate building that had seemed glamorous at first was starting to feel ominously garish, its colors oversaturated and too bright, like we were living in a carnival funhouse rigged with trapdoors.

Now with Charles and all his gear, we usually took the elevator. But that required walking past the stairs.

It worked best if he was buckled into his stroller, or if Tim were carrying him, or if he were strapped to Tim. In those cases, I could simply avoid looking at the stairs as we walked by. But if I was carrying Charles in my arms, it was a problem. I had to stay far away, up against the opposite wall, and walk by quickly, and not even think about the stairs, so as not to be seized with some insane impulse to hold him out over the rail and let him go.

It gave me no joy to take these measures, but they were necessary and important. Keeping quiet about them was also important: I was receiving highly sensitive information on a private line. Lately I felt that there were things I couldn't tell Tim, or tell anyone for that matter. Who in the world would want to hear them?

"You hold him," I would say to Tim as we prepped for an errand. "No, you take him. It's nothing. Here."

WITH TIM BUSY AT WORK, MY MOTHER FLEW OUT TO HELP. IT WAS spring break, traditionally a week of drinking, vacationing, and oblivion-seeking for the faculty. But she had generously foregone all that to come sit in a one-bedroom apartment with me and Charles, handing us bottles and burp cloths.

An anthropology professor, she was not much inclined to tell me how to be a mother. There were countless variations on infant care. I could have wrapped Charles in seal fur or carried him across a raging river in a straw basket, fed him pureed fish or raw goat milk, and for all I knew she wouldn't have made a peep.

Still, she seemed quite taken with Charles, her first grandchild. In this we were like any two women, able to sit and talk for hours about his coloring, his features, his dexterity, his smile, his intelligence, his patterns of feeding and defecation, and whether we knew of a suitable wife, the answer being no (we were not aware of any baby good enough to be his wife), but we would keep an eye out.

By tacit mutual agreement, we treated Charles as the first boy in the family. There were comparisons to me, but none to David, who had died suddenly from a high fever at nineteen months. I knew him by one framed photo, a pretty, dark-haired boy, laughing as he held his hands wide for an unseen ball. My parents seldom mentioned him, and as a child I sensed him only indirectly: waves of relief coming off my father as I continued to be a girl, to grow older, to be different; an abstracted quality in my mother, as if, owing to this same difference, she could not quite see me.

Fortunately, Charles looked nothing like David but was fair like Tim. We needed him to be a fresh, untragic start, and for this part he was well-suited: a golden baby, a good baby.

Nor did we talk about my father, who had been dark-skinned, foreign-born, a professor in the same department as my mother before a fatal heart attack at forty-five. They'd met in graduate school and, by middle age, were distantly cordial housemates: Claudia a tenured workhorse with a long list of committee jobs and publications, her Indian husband, who taught classes in a thick accent, merely tolerated. He was considered odd, prone to tangents, professionally unsavvy. He pocketed leaves from the campus bushes and dropped them into whatever was cooking on the stove. He chuckled at his own untranslatable jokes.

"He was a misfit in this country," Claudia remarked tersely, weeks after he died. "He never adapted, never learned how to play the game." At twelve, I took in this information and said nothing. Claudia was now my only parent, and in her scattered remarks I tried to discern some sort of guidance.

Still, he had been fond of me, this peculiar occupant of my mother's world, and in his final years, I wondered if I might be like him in some way. Not long before his death, I observed him from a distance, walking a long diagonal path across the campus: a slight brown man in a brown suit carrying an old-fashioned briefcase, his face obscured by drugstore sunglasses. A lonely figure.

"How about a chocolate martini?" said Tim.

"I really shouldn't," said Claudia.

"Come on, live a little!"

"Fine. Just one."

Replicating a drink from a hotel bar we had been to on Claudia's first visit, Tim mixed Godiva chocolate, crème de cacao, and vodka and served it in two martini glasses. I was still nursing and abstained. The dinner dishes cleared, Claudia had moved a puzzle board to the dining room table and was piecing together a wintry scene. I had just put Charles to bed.

"To science!" said Tim, lifting his glass.

"To science!" we repeated, smiling.

He had just received a promotion from general assignment reporter to science and technology reporter, his own beat. A pre-med major before switching to journalism, Tim had a mind for science. He didn't want to do it himself—pure research was too incremental, too niggling—but he had a hobbyist's enthusiasm for developments in physics, computing, genetics, and astronomy: the stuff of sci-fi, potential game-changers for the human race. With its universities and labs, its burgeoning technology industry and start-ups, the city was rich in such news.

"Congratulations," Claudia said warmly. "I can't wait to read your new stories, though I liked the old ones, too."

"Ah, well," said Tim. "Hopefully they won't be too boring." He and my mother got along, and at times he seemed to solicit her approval. His own faraway mother was stingy with affection. She seemed to view Tim as a ne'er-do-well who didn't become a doctor or some other high-earning type, letting the family down. To Claudia, however, Tim was the smart, good boy who married her daughter, an offbeat daughter whose charms were an acquired taste.

"There is a purity to science," Claudia mused. "So much of my own field, in the so-called social sciences, is driven by intellectual trends, but you've either found a new star or you haven't. An invention either works or it doesn't. It's refreshing."

"Don't kid yourself," said Tim. "There's plenty of politics involved. That's one of the aspects I find fascinating: the personalities, the players."

"Getting funding is very political, I imagine."

"Absolutely. It's all who you know. The peer review system is not a meritocracy as one might think. The entire 'scientific method' is in a way a polite fiction."

"I think I'll have some juice," I announced, getting up. "Do we have any orange juice?"

"No, we're out," said Tim. "I think you're giving anthropology short shrift…"

I drifted into the kitchen and poured myself a glass of milk. In the background, Claudia and Tim seemed engaged in a contest to out-compliment each other's fields. When I returned to the dining room, Claudia was saying, "It's one thing to study a reality created by humans, a particular culture shaped by economics, geography, even the weather—a contingent reality. But there is something to be said for a changeless, *in*human—"

"Oh, I don't know," Tim interjected.

"—reality, woven into the very fabric of the world and waiting there to be discovered."

"Yes, but isn't it a bit cold?" Tim swirled the chocolatey dregs in his glass. "The human layer that makes meaning out of the material world—isn't that more worthy of study, in a way?"

"They're complementary realities," Claudia offered professorially. "The material and the cultural, in constant dynamic interplay—"

"What about the evil eye?" I piped up.

"What?"

"Remember that story about the evil eye?"

"Oh, Cara. I'm surprised you even remember that."

"The evil what?" Tim asked.

Claudia began, sounding bemused, or like she was trying to sound bemused:

Long ago, on a trip to India with my father, she'd heard a story about a village girl who travelled to the city to visit her husband's family. Young and beautiful, the bride excited jealousy among the servants. Her in-laws put them up in an expensive hotel, in a high-up room with a balcony where she could look over the city.

The young couple had been married about a year and had their baby with them. One morning while her husband showered, the girl felt a strange compulsion to take the baby out of his crib and bring him onto the balcony. For no reason she could begin to explain, she approached the edge. This same compulsion, now very strong, caused her to hold the baby over the balcony rail, one hand at his head and the other at his ankles.

"All she had to do," said Claudia, "was go like this"—she drew her upturned palms apart a few inches—"and the baby would fall to his death. Strange as it may sound, it took every ounce of her willpower not to do this. She had to physically make herself hold on to him. She stood there for several seconds, and finally pulled him in and took him back inside."

"Whoa," said Tim.

"She was of course horrified at her own behavior. It happened two more times—"

"Are you *kidding* me?"

"—before she finally told her mother-in-law, in tears, what she had done. The mother-in-law knew at once what had happened. 'Someone has given you the evil eye,' she said. It was likely one of the servants: an old woman who had been at the house the day before the

46

compulsions started. The mother-in-law brought a red pepper from the kitchen. She slowly circled it three times around the girl's face, muttering certain words. I don't know what they were. When she was done, she threw the pepper into the fire where it burned up, creating smoke but no smell whatsoever. The girl went back to the hotel and never had the urge again."

"It was some kind of curse?" said Tim after a pause.

"That's what your dad believed," said Claudia, looking at me. "Of course, he would say that. He was always superstitious. Years ago, I spent some time studying the 'evil eye' as a transcultural phenomenon, common across peasant societies. I was planning to write an article about it, but I could never quite understand how…" She trailed off. "I guess it's just one of those things. I had several other projects going at the time, and the subject was tangential to my research."

"That's a crazy story all right," Tim said. "But what does it have to do with science?"

"Nothing," I answered. "That's my point. There's no good explanation."

"Claudia?" said Tim. "You okay?"

"Oh, fine," my mother said, suddenly weary. "It's getting late, that's all. I think it's time to—"

"When did you hear this story again?" I asked sharply. Tim shot me a quizzical look. "What year was it?"

She thought a moment, then answered with a later year than I'd expected.

"So, you and Dad were already married," I pressed. "In fact, wasn't David born that year?"

Did Claudia flinch, or did I just imagine it? It was so quick, just a microexpression. Anyone else would have called it a blink, but I was watching her face. Evenly, she said, "Yes, I suppose he was."

"He would've been what, four months old? Why were they travelling with a baby?"

"Oh, I don't know, Cara. We might have had some project overseas. Remember, we were still in school. Maybe we'd taken a detour to show the baby to Dad's family. It was more than thirty years ago. I barely remember that trip. There were so many. Anyway, it's getting late. I should get back to my hotel. Timothy, would you mind calling me a cab?"

I took this in like the reporter I once was: the human news. With a shock, I realized one part of the story was a lie. There was no village girl.

Why hadn't I seen it before, the image now clear in my mind's eye: Claudia as a slender young woman, her hair in a loose ponytail, her pale arms stretched over the drop, an unseen figure on a balcony pitched over the din and smog of a foreign city. Her mouth set in a line, she was concentrating on her two hands: one at the baby's head, the other at his ankles. Her grip was loose, the child relaxed. She struggled not to move, dimly aware of doing wrong. *Pull him in. You have to pull him in, right now.* Long seconds passed until the baby made a sound, piercing her trance just enough to allow her to pull him in. That was the first time.

As Tim walked Claudia to the door, I closed my eyes and sat perfectly still. "Night, Mom."

She was in town for one more day, and we spent many hours together with the baby. I could have told her—I thought of telling her—I couldn't walk past the stairs. But we didn't really have those kinds of conversations.

With some effort, I could control my symptoms, if that's what they were. I found Charles's presence calming. Smiling at me in a Li'l Slugger shirt with mashed banana on his face, he radiated pure trust. I drank it in. Finding I didn't like sharp knives as well as stairs, I left the big blades in the sink for Tim to clean. It was a matter of taking a few steps back, walking away, to render dirty knives benign.

This was all doable.

Information was coming in on a rare frequency, staticky as a distant radio transmission. Its sense-flashes and wordless messages were cryptic, incomplete. I could have dulled it or ignored it, but it was all of pressing interest: news from the outer edges of my own capacities. It told me to be careful, and I very much wanted to be careful.

My only similar experience took place in my freshman year of college. I was at a faraway school, not Yale but a brand name, noteworthy for someone from my hometown, which was only a tiny dot marked on the paper-flat plains of flyover country. My first semester had gone well, the dizzying whirl I expected, but on returning to my cell-like dorm in January, I felt something inside me jangle and unlatch.

I began doing certain things over and over, like playing an old cassette of Ella Fitzgerald songs. Her lilting, smiling voice wanted to reassure me. But after weeks of Ella's tireless efforts, I was no more reassured.

By spring, it was becoming difficult to leave my room. Crossing the campus—an idyll of moss-covered buildings, green lawns, and footbridges over meandering brooks—filled me with dread. It took enormous effort to walk to class and back, but once inside a covered building, I was safe. Researching this condition, I learned it had its own name: agoraphobia.

Meanwhile, final papers were being assigned. These required me to talk about something, anything, for twenty pages with no betrayal of abnormality. For my favorite spring class, I chose to discuss Tennyson's poetry…in which most major characters, I now realized to my amazement, had agoraphobia. Take Mariana, who languished "all day within the dreamy house":

When thickest dark did trance the sky,
She drew her casement-curtain by
And glanced athwart the glooming flats.

Or, take The Lady of Shalott, who spent her nights and days weaving in a tower, cursed if she so much as glanced down to Camelot. Even Tennyson's eagle, a nameless bird in a six-line poem, seemed nauseated as he "clasp[ed] the crag with crooked hands." He didn't want to be there any more than I did.

The wrinkled sea beneath him crawls—

How sickening. Go inside, eagle!

I printed out twenty-three pages of "'All Day Within the Dreamy House: Tennyson and the Agoraphobic Imagination," stapled it, clutched it to my chest, and staggered with heroic resolve across campus to deliver it. Back in my dorm at last, I played more Ella and did not leave my room for thirty-six hours.

I got an *A* on the paper.

The following week, I flew home and never went back.

Instead, I finished my B.A. at the local state teacher's college, where I was celebrated, as if a unicorn had wandered onto campus, for genuinely wanting to read books. After graduation, I moved three hours away to replace the retiring City Hall reporter at a small weekly paper.

By late spring, Tim and I were tired and cranky. Charles still spent nights in our bed. Though his bassinet was an arm's reach away, he slept in it fitfully, aware of his exile, and only when I scooped him out and snuggled him close could we both sleep.

None of us, though, slept very well. Each night brought night feedings, night kickings, night wails that came out of nowhere, Charles barreling out of a dream like an action hero against some hellish backdrop. Soon Tim's alarm clock would go off, making him groan and me obscurely angry. The fact that he had to get up and go to work was strangely irritating, while the fact that I got to stay in bed seemed to irritate *him*.

During the day, I got the baby fed and dressed and myself showered and groomed. The amount of time this took was glacial, prehistoric. Whole eras passed outside our windows; species evolved, reproduced fifty generations, and died out before I had my shoes on. Breakfast plans turned into lunch plans and finally into staying home, thumbing through an old decorating magazine for hours. Square chartreuse pillows danced before my eyes. We seemed to lack for many things: mohair throws, candles. Finally, I'd toss the rag aside. Was Tim due yet? No, it was only two.

This must be motherhood, I gathered: this epic and mythical solitude, aloneness so complete that it was like a spell cast in a fairy tale. No one had told me what to expect, nor hinted since Charles's birth that anything was amiss. No one had said, *Where is your family, your mother, your friends? Why have they left you all alone?* So I didn't think anything of it. In the endless hours, weird new thoughts circled and re-circled like a school of silver fish in the eerie silence of the ocean's depths.

On sunny afternoons, I'd take us upstairs to the roof deck, where an assortment of lawn furniture had been abandoned to collective use. Some tenants had put out pots of flowers or herbs, so there was often someone puttering around or taking in the view over the long, red terra cotta wall. The roof deck didn't make me nervous because we stayed well in its center: Charles dozing in the stroller's shaded interior, buckled and safe; me in sunglasses, gazing into the searing brightness of the city's sky.

Tim could be gone up to ten hours. When he walked in the door at night, I handed off our child like a quarterback in a running play and retreated into the kitchen or a locked bathroom just because I could. The quality of dinner varied greatly: one night, Irish stew and homemade soda bread, the next a clump of pasta with sauce from a jar, the third a vacant look, the fourth a batch of festive cupcakes and a wedge of cheese.

Over our plates, Tim told me all about his day. He seemed to want something from me—murmurs of validation or motherly pride—that after all day home with Charles, seemed like an awful lot to ask. "Mmm hmm," I'd respond. "Wow. That's great." Meanwhile, some rageful inner flame blazed into being. Tim jawed on about his editors, sources, and competition. I was tired, yet he insisted on tiring me more.

"Can you just stop?" I interrupted one night. "Can you please just…stop talking."

Tim stopped. He looked surprised. "What? Why?"

In less than five minutes, the evening went completely off the rails. I seized the dirty plates and flung them clattering into the sink. Tim kicked a cupboard and bellowed obscenities till the walls shook. From some subversive hiding place, a pack of cigarettes materialized, and as he defiantly raised one to his lips, I threatened to call the landlord, the pediatrician, both our mothers. Every toxic, half-formed thought I'd ever had came flying out, thrilling and terrible. With bags under his eyes and a lit Marlboro clamped between his teeth, Tim appeared to have aged ten years since the last time I really looked at him.

"Is this how you want to behave, Cara, in front of your own *child?*" he snapped.

I stood there with nothing to say. I had forgotten about Charles. Ten feet away, he squirmed inside a wicker basket. He'd been asleep but now regarded me with bright, wide-open eyes as I stood over him, experiencing a cold tremor of horror.

I'd wanted to protect him from everything in the wide, wicked world. But I could not even protect him from myself.

7

JUST BACK FROM GROUP THERAPY AT MILDRED W., TEN OF US SEATED in a circle in a large room with mint-green walls. The therapist seems very young, but I find myself wanting to impress her, to raise my hand and give correct answers to her questions. The other patients are a motley bunch in varying stages of psychic disintegration, humming or shuffling or staring off into space. Being around them makes me feel crystalline and razor-sharp, a paragon of reason. Surely, she can see how alike we are, both college-educated women? In some other context, we could be friends. I would ask about her work at the hospital, and she would ask how things were going at home. If we were real friends, could I explain things better?

As it is, each day I find that I have less and less to say. I want to give her the right answers, but she's asking the wrong questions. Ever so gently, in language laced with tact and compassion, she is suggesting that the problem is inside of me. What in my history, what immediate stressors, have hindered my ability to adapt, to thrive? Her frame of reference, the personal psychodrama, is the size of a postage stamp, a cinematic tight shot that doesn't capture the big picture.

Does she have children? I noted first thing that her ring finger is bare. She probably goes home to her roommate or her dog. What does she know about my life? So far, she's done all the same things as the guys—college, internships, job—keeping up easily at every step. She doesn't understand yet how the city turns on you when you do something messily female: have a baby. How it isolates you and tries to pry you away from your own child, to put you back on the clock and generating income. The city sees your infant as a hindrance, a drag on the system, to be stashed with some minimum-wage worker as soon as possible so you can get back with the program. And for what? The honor of renting an overpriced apartment? The privilege of standing in line outside the Apple Store for this year's model? *The city is doing this to me,* I want to say. *The city is crazy.* And that isn't the only problem, just the first one, the easier one. I don't know how to talk about the second, which is not limited to the city at all. The stomach-lurch of vertigo has deepened, no longer specific to the stairs but as if the whole world sits on a broad plane that has imperceptibly tilted. Beyond the plane's furthest edge, an abyss gapes, a black infinity of nothingness. Nobody else seems to perceive this, but it is never far from my mind.

"Cara? How about you?" the therapist asked this morning, piercing my ruminative fog. "Can you think of a time when it would have been helpful to pause and count to ten, or practice mindfulness?"

One, two, three, four. I took a deep breath, inhaling banality and exhaling it back into the room in a great cleansing gust.

"Pass," I said.

AN EMBARRASSING THING HAPPENED AFTER THERAPY. I HAD TO WASH my clothes.

After several days in my jeans and T-shirt, I felt grimy and vaguely shameful, in violation of my own low standards.

I never cared much about clothes, but then, I didn't really need to. I realize now that, for most of my life, I looked good in everything. Whatever "body insecurities" I had before having kids seem laughable: a buzzing beehive of neuroses gifted to me by the culture at large. I was a healthy young woman with a girlish figure I'd never have again, but my mind was littered with anxious phrases like *clean eating* and *skinny fat*, with *flat stomach* and *thigh gap*. Too late, I now understand that, during those years, I looked amazing. I should have worn short skirts and tight sweaters and sashayed down the street! Instead, I had dressed like a timid nerd. And now, I dressed like what I was: a mom.

Still, until this week, my clothes were at least clean. I packed no suitcase for the psych ward, not even a toothbrush or a change of underwear.

"We have a laundry room," an orderly remarked to me at lunch. "If a machine is free, you're welcome to use it. There's a bottle of detergent on the shelf." She wore whimsical scrubs, a matching top and bottom in a Mickey Mouse print, and they looked comfortable and soft from many launderings. I envied her.

"Oh, okay. Great. Where is it?"

She sketched out a route down the hall, around a corner, past the nurses' station. "Someone can loan you a gown," she added, "to wear while you wait."

I nodded, not fully understanding. What she meant was, I would have to kill a few hours nearly nude. While my clothes churned with agonizing slowness through the laundry cycle, I had to get back to my room in nothing but two flimsy hospital gowns, one tied backward around my waist for modesty.

Hot-faced with shame, I inched along the wall. Hospital staff averted their eyes as they passed. Assorted patients walked by in street clothes, beltless and shoeless but otherwise unremarkable urban dwellers. They could be getting lunch downtown or hanging off straps on the subway. For the most part, the psychiatric ward looks like a city street: a parade of scruffy loners, heads down, preoccupied with themselves.

I, on the other hand, look naked, lost, and unfit for society. My hair is frizzy and unkempt, my eyes ringed in dark circles from poor sleep. My expression as I slunk through the ward was feral, hunted—mainly because I have no pants, but also because my sense of identity is dissipating, leaking out, like a balloon deflating.

Now I'm hunkered down in my room, dreading the return trip to the laundry. I feel on edge, disoriented. Why am I here, stuck in a hospital, wearing hospital clothes?

I used to be a newspaper reporter. A copy editor. A girlfriend, then a wife. A mother. Everything about my situation whispers what I am now.

I'm ill.

8

WITH TIM BACK AT WORK AFTER THE BIRTH, I SPENT MOST MY TIME with Charles and the cat. This was my longtime companion, predating Tim; in fact, I'd left her home alone to go on our first date. Though Tim initially found her ridiculous, he'd warmed up to her over time, and now she belonged to us both, a valued member of the family.

Mew was a Himalayan with long white hair and orange tips on her ears and tail. With her squashed face and downturned mouth, she looked like a high-maintenance pet, but of all of us, she was the most stoic and uncomplaining. Despite her name, she rarely made a sound. She liked to wedge herself into a small space like a shoebox, casting a watery blue gaze on the goings-on in our rooms. Often she fell asleep, which seemed an obscure comment or critique.

In all my years with Mew, she'd been an indoor cat. No one who tried to imagine her outdoors could do it; it was impossible to picture anything but instant bloody death. This sensitive creature was not made for the urban rough-and-tumble, or any rough or any tumble whatsoever. Her only functions were ornamental and spiritual: the higher functions.

Before we'd moved to the city, Mew had no experience living high off the ground, and I never entirely trusted her not to jump out a window. It was important to keep her confined to 3C, because if she ever escaped the building, she was as good as gone. Yet once, after Charles was born and we were less vigilant, cat-wise, she must have slipped out the front door as we fussed with the diaper bag or stroller. A tense hour ensued as we searched for her all over the building, Charles slung over my shoulder, Tim and I calling her name as if she answered to it.

Finally, I went home with the baby, leaving Tim the thankless task of casing the block. I knew my cat was gone forever and in this desolate state barely heard the door. I wasn't sure it was a knock, but seconds later it came louder, three sharp raps. I opened the door, and before me stood a small, wizened person in owlish glasses, cradling Mew like a baby.

"I believe this belongs to you?" she said.

It was the Old Woman, whose real name was Tabitha Brown.

"Oh wow! Thank you! Where'd you find her? Come here, Mew! Thank you so much."

"I was folding my laundry," she said, enunciating with verve, "when I felt something rubbing against my leg. Well, I nearly jumped out of my skin! But when I looked down, it was this beautiful kitty. I picked her up and read her tag, and sadly knew I couldn't keep her, much as I'd like to."

From the basket on the coffee table where I'd dumped him, Charles let out a cry.

"You have a baby in here, too?"

"Yes, come on in. I just need to pick him up. My name's Cara."

I scooped up Charles and cleared off a chair. When Tim walked in the door some ten minutes later, we were still chatting.

"Well, I couldn't—whoa. She's right here."

"Oh, Tim! I'm sorry. I forgot to call you. This is Tabitha. She lives one floor down and across the hall. She found Mew in the laundry room and brought her back!"

"Ms. Brown? I've seen your name on the door buzzer. Nice to meet you."

The next week, Tabitha invited us to tea in her apartment. "It's nothing fancy," she warned. "I just buy cookies and things and set them out."

"We'd love to come to tea," I said. Since having Charles, my social circle had collapsed to a pinpoint. Tim still had his friends at work, but I was home all day surrounded by retirees, freelancers, loners: apartment people. None of them showed much interest in me or the baby, but Tabitha was different. She was a mother, for one thing, though her two sons were middle-aged.

Wearing a bright-colored scarf around her shoulders, she ushered us into her apartment with little cries of joy, like we were honored guests. The living room was dimmer than ours and filled with heavy furniture whose tops were crowded with photographs, books, and magazines. Framed paintings—actual paintings, their textured surfaces daubed by human hands—hung over side tables and ceramic lamps. At one end of a massive, claw-footed table, she had laid out tea for three.

"Saturday," Tim read on his porcelain teacup. "And Saturday it is."

"Thursday," I read. "A few days early."

"I like to use this day-of-week set," said Tabitha, whose cup said Tuesday. "Though I always thought there should be two cups for each day, so you could have tea with someone and be accurate."

"That would make for an unwieldy set," said Tim.

"Yes, I suppose you're right. Well, cheers."

Tabitha hailed from an old theater family. Born to some wealth, her father had been an actor and her mother had run a dance studio. Tabitha had trained there and, in her twenties, toured the world as a modern dancer, running with an avant-garde crowd. They held transgressive political opinions, attended protests, were fluent in multiple languages, partied, danced. Some years ago, she'd sold the family house and attached studio, by that time worth a mint in the city, and now lived quietly among her things and memories, an apartment person.

"My younger son keeps an eye on me," Tabitha said wryly. "He lives close by and stops in every few weeks to make sure I'm still kicking. You'd like him, Tim. He works at the university in geology."

Her older son, who lived overseas, was a "jack-of-all-trades."

After learning Tabitha's history, Tim and I sketched ours, which seemed comparatively bland. Tim described his job at the newspaper; I expounded on life with Charles. Tabitha seemed delighted by it all.

"He's an absolutely marvelous baby," she pronounced. "Look at him: so alert, so intelligent. Well done."

We left with smiles and waves, promising to come back soon. I for one meant it. The city was teeming with people, but it was hard to make a friend.

IT WAS NOW SUMMERTIME, AND CHARLES HAD BEEN WITH US HALF A year. He laughed, sat up, felt hefty and substantial in my arms. He did "tummy time" on a mat with his toys. Charles was thrilled by many things: baths, Scotch tape, wooden blocks. He was a vivid little person, full of energy and life.

He had a new stroller with big wheels for jogging, and almost every day we'd roll into the elevator and out the lobby door. I still had fleeting anxious thoughts. At times, my surroundings seemed to shimmer and ripple like the surface of a lake, three dimensions compressed into a thin shining film concealing something bigger, deeper. But things seemed better in the summer with its balmy days, the light lemon-drop yellow. I was ready to shed excess baby weight and baggy winter clothes, so we spent hours trekking the sidewalks and the looping path around the lake.

Our walks were full of words, stories the city told about itself: a sticker on a graffiti-tagged parking meter (BROKE), a company name on a T-shirt (*Quotidian Enterprises*), a tattoo across a woman's bare dark back (*My mama raised me well so I rebel*). Like two spies hiding in plain sight, Charles and I wended our bulky way through the city's coffee shops, stores, and parks, catching snippets of conversation.

A middle-aged guy talking to his buddy over bagels: "So, this kid comes to see me about a fine he has for a late book. He tells me he got arrested last week, and the book was in his backpack."

A girl as pale and delicate as an Edward Gorey figure, phone pressed to her ear: "No. No. You're not listening. I didn't say that. You didn't hear what I said."

"He said he asked the booking officer to send the book back to the library, and they said they would. Maybe they sent it to another library. Who knows where they sent it?"

"I don't know why I even talk to you, since you don't listen to what I say! I didn't say you were making me sick."

"So, I told the kid—nice kid—'We'll wait another few weeks without fining you and see if anybody sends it in.'"

"No. No! I'd never say that. I said you weren't helping me get *better*."

"But what I wanted to tell him was, 'You're obviously so stoned out of your mind right now, there's no way you're even going to remember this conversation.'"

"Shut up, shut up. Just leave me alone!"

The trick of living in the city was not to treat people like things. Not like vending machines that gave you stuff for money, not like blights on the landscape or obstacles in your path, not like noisemakers interfering with your enjoyment of a movie, but like unique and complex beings fully equal to yourself. I knew this and yet found it hard to do in practice. There were too many of them; the human mind could not trot out to meet each like a friendly dog but remained crouched and wary in its lair, constantly primed for fight-or-flight. Thus a tableau of threats, inconveniences, and human props or design elements arrayed itself before you at all times, moving and changing like a video game where reflexes were key. Having a baby here required the radical dialing-back of every instinct, as instead of being surrounded by wise and capable aunts and guarded by a throng of warrior-males, I paraded my infant through crowds of strangers every day, entirely alone, with nothing between him and a four-lane street but a few feet of blistered pavement.

As I leaned into Charles's stroller for the uphill push back to our building, an old woman who sometimes lurked in the crevice between the tanning salon and Ethiopian restaurant muttered as we passed. I only caught the last few words: "— your f——ing t—s off!"

There were days when everyone looked homeless, and today was one of those days. Everyone on the city's streets looked raggedy and demented. Old, young, white, black, single or in groups, driving SUVs with yin/yang bumper stickers or striding backpacked down the sidewalk, everyone looked lost, unwell, and vaguely malevolent.

"We have a problem," Tim said.

"Oh? Do tell."

We were sometimes getting along and sometimes not. It hardly mattered, as this was a new day with new work to be done. Now the logistics of our lives required close cooperation; there was no other way to do it, so we were learning to put our quarrels aside and just get back to work. We had a certain new maturity, in a galley-slave way.

"The Man Downstairs complained to the landlord about us."

"Isn't he dead?"

"No. That was the old Man Downstairs. The new one is a real piece of work. We've run into him a few times. Colin, Ewan, some pretentious-sounding—"

"*Lachlan Keene?* That guy lives under us now? Great."

Lachlan Keene was a graduate student, about 6'4" with red hair, a pale sensitive face, and glasses. In another life I might have been strangely attracted to him, but I now felt a rogue desire to poison him. He had previously lived in another unit in the building and invited us in once, when we still enjoyed a cordial relationship. His apartment was like something out of a Kubrick film: insanely sterile, freakishly austere. He had an antique baseball worth $25K in a glass case.

"Not to state the obvious," I said. "But this would be the perfect opportunity to break into his apartment and steal his baseball."

"He's keeping some kind of log," said Tim.

"All we have to do is scale the building from our window to his window. I wonder if he leaves his windows unlocked. It's three floors up, why lock them? He's keeping what? What kind of log?"

"Every time we make a noise, he writes it down, along with the time and his theory of what caused it. It's very meticulous, apparently. Shelley just called and told me all about it."

Shelley was the owner of our building, a regal, expensively dressed black woman who never returned our calls. The fact that she'd called us seemed like some kind of honor, but also ominous.

"What did you tell her?"

"I told her all we do is walk around. The baby's up at night, so we're up. She told me to stop wearing shoes. I'll wear shoes in my own house if I want to."

"I didn't realize we were noisy. I guess we can be more careful. Lachlan, I'm sure, is like the Princess and the Pea, but we can try. Have you given any thought," I added blandly, "to just killing him and taking his baseball?"

"I have to go to work. And you, young man, keep it down, will ya?"

"We could really use the money." I was leaning into the riff. If people really were just things, all was permitted and Lachlan Keene a mere obstacle in our path. "Come on. Aren't you feeling adventurous?"

"No dice," said Tim.

I sighed. Our prior downstairs neighbor never bothered us. He quietly drank himself to death, his body undiscovered for days. I missed that guy.

WHEN I THINK OF ALL THAT HAPPENED LATER, I DON'T KNOW WHO OR what to blame. Tim and I were nice people, really, and the things we wanted were good. But it was quickly becoming clear we couldn't afford life in the city, and a materialist would say that was the root cause of our problems. We couldn't afford a bigger place, therefore we couldn't sleep, therefore, despite our best intentions, everything began to erode. The city was the basket in which we had placed all our eggs, only to find it did not care about us, nor even particularly like us.

We were trying to do a big job: the job of being a human family. But the city had other jobs in mind, jobs it encouraged and exalted: operations consultant, tax attorney, cosmetic dermatologist, data entry clerk.

IT WAS OUR FIRST SUMMER WITH CHARLES AND, IN DAZED GRATITUDE, we spent our weekends taking him on outings. We took him to the beach and marveled at the grains of sand between his toes. We took him to the space museum, feeling wonder that human beings just like Charles had made it into orbit, even to the moon. We took him swimming; we slid down red plastic slides holding him on our laps. At a train crossing we said, "Look, Charles!" and waved at the train. We bought him his own bowl of ice cream and laughed at his surprise at the coldness on his tongue.

We drove two hours to take him to the zoo, where Charles rode high on Tim's shoulders in a floppy hat. I glanced up every few seconds to see his expression, which was open-mouthed and staring, as if he were viewing an ordinary dog. On some level we knew it was foolish to take a baby to the zoo: Charles had never seen a Pomeranian, so what extra was gained by showing him a tiger? He was delighted by a sneeze, so how could he appreciate the ingenious adaptation of the kangaroo? A tree, a sparrow, an empty yogurt container were new and exotic to Charles, so why take him to see an elephant? At this point, everything was elephants.

We ourselves were stunned by the zoo. Charles was living in a world of wonders. If he could only understand the intricate, impossible beauty of the place we were trying, somewhat ham-handedly, to show him. But nobody could fully understand it, neither us nor Charles. We were a little higher up the ladder than he was, but that was all.

"Look, Charles," said Tim. "It's an okapi!" This was my favorite version of Tim: a knowledgeable, doting dad. Sometimes I couldn't remember why we fought so much.

"They're in the giraffe family," I said, looping an arm around Tim's waist.

"They live in Africa." Tim slung his left arm over my shoulders, his right hand holding Charles's leg.

"They are essentially solitary, coming together only to breed," I read. "I've never heard of them before. Have you?"

"Nope. They're beautiful, though."

"They are. Oh, Charles, he's looking right at you!"

We were trying to hold onto something, to shield it from forces we could neither see nor describe. Something surrounded us that had no name, but we had gotten its attention. It was moving closer. Tim and I sensed we had a fragile, precious thing, if only we could keep it.

9

I HAD STOPPED GOING TO THE MOVIES. THE OLD ART DECO THEATER down the hill, an ornate historic landmark with a marquis that displayed showtimes in gold lights, was now merely a building I walked past with Charles on our daily pilgrimage to Anywhere But 3C. I barely noticed what was playing. The glossy posters I'd once collected to show off my taste now seemed irrelevant as my sandals slapped the pavement. My hands gripped the stroller bar as I continually scanned our surroundings. On a moment's notice, I was ready to unbuckle Charles and throw him into a metal trash can in the event of a dog attack, willing to take on a menacing vagrant in hand-to-hand combat if it came to that.

Say what you will about my life, it was no longer flat; with motherhood, it had exploded into three dimensions. Inside the theater, some ghostly former version of myself was opening a reporter's notebook and gazing at the screen, waiting for the main event to start. But out here in the vivid present, on the pavement, it had started. I walked past storefronts and cafés, nail salons and sports bars, pushing the baby through an endless array of consumer choices. High on an elegant old building, bas-relief images of toddlers—the plump, serene faces of cherubs—hovered above the city's pedestrians, but few of us were looking up. At ground-level, it was all signs and ads, a random series of mascots, slogans, and catchphrases, and the occasional street-side trash can, filled to overflowing.

Where is the beauty I was promised? This question darted through my mind, born of some wild, inchoate feeling. Raised in a town of unrelenting drabness—a hodgepodge of squat municipal offices, ugly banks, plasticky fast-food drive-ups, every public building a copy of a copy of something that might have been okay but now seemed fake and out-of-place—I always thought the city would be better. Movies were set in cities, after all. Exciting and romantic, sparkling with lights, cities were backdrops against which lives of significance could be lived.

In my hometown, everything seemed dull and insipid, but somewhere, I believed, beauty existed and beckoned, like Oz. During my high school years, I studied the poster tacked to my wall: skyscrapers against a rose-colored sunset; a white bridge, elaborate as lace, piercing the haze; seabirds in flight over a calm and gleaming ocean.

Now I lived in the city and, up close, it didn't look so good. Like a stunned and bedraggled mom, the city had let itself go. Some animating spirit of *joie de vivre* had departed, and now it lumbered along in sweatpants, a surreptitious day drinker.

Had I been duped? Was beauty real, or just a dream conjured up by the movies? Certainly, the high-end shops were filled with pretty clothes. A style I called Bohemian Milkmaid was in every boutique window: flowery dresses, Victorian hairpins, midriff-baring blouses with puffed sleeves, whimsical motifs of songbirds and umbrellas, lace-up boots with pointy toes, gold lockets. You'd think the average city girl spent her days in a garden, sipping lavender tea from a scalloped cup, not parked in front of a screen ten floors off the ground, breathing recirculated air, the windows bolted shut so as to prevent suicides. Some airy fantasy of beauty and refinement still moved merchandise, but the effect was one of pampered children playing dress-up. Anyway, all of it was too pricey for me.

What about the Great Outdoors? There was beauty to be found there, an hour or two outside the city. In our pre-Charles lives, Tim and I had huffed down many a trail, consumed sandwiches on many a windswept bluff. I had no great love for nature—where I grew up, nature was tumbleweeds and roadkill—but I liked getting away from people. The white noise of a river or a waterfall drowned my thoughts, allowing me to simply be, like a lizard baking on a rock.

In fact, escaping the city was the city's most sought-after pastime, perhaps even its highest civic value. People came back to work with rapturous tales of vacation, the rest of us listening wide-eyed, mute with longing, as they described near-empty beaches where the surf crashed like a god, dappled forests stirring with ancient magic, snow-covered mountaintops overlooking primeval lands untouched by human feet: all the places they'd fled to, at great expense and effort, as if to cancel out the city by mathematical negation. Forced to explain his absence from the office, my boss Ben, the only person I knew with real money, would sheepishly cop to the fact that he'd been on a two-week walking tour of Ireland or taking daily saunas with a majestic view of the fjords. Was *this* the beauty to be found out in the world? If so, I'd missed out and was likely to keep missing out, forever.

Maybe this was why people went to the movies. But even that was off the table for a while.

More than an hour into my walk, the afternoon sun was beating down. The long, warm ride had lulled Charles to sleep. I stopped and pushed open a door to the tinkle of bells, feeling a mix of apprehension and resignation. This was one of our usual haunts, a hole-in-the-wall restaurant on an undistinguished block, located at the point in our miles-long walk at which I felt the urge to sit down. The place was decked out in bright-colored cantina kitsch: plastic flowers, decorative blankets, and sombreros. A mariachi band sang lustily from a wall-mounted speaker. As usual, at midafternoon, the dining area was empty. An eerie stillness hung over it like a curse.

I rolled the stroller up to the counter where, behind the cash register, the proprietress, Paloma, lurked like a death's head. A gaunt, middle-aged woman with ice-blonde hair, she was always there, clacking her nails, baring a rictus of false teeth. For ten hours a day, six days a week, she stood at her post, waiting to encounter the next customer on whom to pass a wordless, terrible judgment.

"What you like today, honey?" Paloma inquired in her high-handed way.

Her sharp gaze swept over Charles and me. I met her eyes as complex waves of female data passed between us. From a faded news clipping on the wall, I'd gleaned that she'd run the restaurant for decades. Although they weren't evident in the cantina, which was staffed only by Paloma and one cowed, sad-eyed kitchen boy, I sensed there had been children once. A husband. Running the movie reel backward, it was easy to see Paloma as a glamorous and ambitious young woman, ready to work around the clock and have it all. But over time, the faithless husband had disappeared; the kids had grown up and moved away. Feisty and proud, she'd poured more and more energy into the business, even as the neighborhood turned seedy and trendy restaurants sprang up two streets away. Always meticulously thin, she was willing to suffer for her looks: nips and tucks, yellowing teeth filed and capped. No one could outwork her, outlast her, or hold herself to higher standards.

Yet here we were: two women alone in the middle of the city. As she summed me up at a glance—friendless, in frumpy clothes, my forehead slick with sweat—I couldn't tell whether she felt pity, contempt, or some mix of the two. Maybe with a dash of baby nostalgia thrown in, tinged with the bitter knowledge that, one day, children would abandon and betray you. Maybe she approved of my long walks— losing weight!—or maybe she despised me for being a $10 table-for-one, barely worth the free chips and salsa the tragic kitchen boy would place on my table before slinking away.

"I'll have the cheese enchilada plate," I peeped.

"What kind of beans?"

"Black."

"Okay."

Paloma handed me a table marker with a number on it, as if there were too many customers to keep straight in her mind. I wheeled the stroller to one of the empty tables, parked it to face my chair, and settled in to wait for my chips.

The restaurant was rather pretty, in its way. It had been decked out to feel like a foreign country, convivial and festive, rich in tradition. It must have reminded Paloma of her home. In this, I envied her a little. No place I went ever reminded me of home. Even my current residence, 3C, didn't feel like a proper home—more like a fragile nest made of twigs and string, perched on a rocky crag that overlooked the city. No style of music called me back to where I came from, who I was.

Deep in his shadowy canvas enclosure, Charles stirred. He unclenched his fists into two tiny starfish and opened his eyes.

"Well, hello!" Instinctively, I smiled and spoke in a musical voice. Trumpets blaring, the mariachi band seemed to kick into a higher gear, energetic and joyful. "Look who's awake!"

The baby focused on my face and waved his arms. His eyes were impossibly blue.

Beautiful blue.

DURING THOSE DAYS WITH CHARLES, I WAS ALWAYS AFRAID. PEOPLE who weren't afraid every waking hour seemed foolish, ostriches with their heads in the sand. Back in my journalism days, I'd read about a young mountain climber known for scaling the highest, most dangerous peaks with his bare hands: not using a pick or even a rope, but simply crawling up a sheer granite face with a 10,000-foot drop. He said he felt calm on the mountain, just him and it. Freeways made him nervous, though. There were "too many variables" he couldn't control: diesel trucks barreling past at 80 miles an hour, teenagers texting at the wheel, every bungler who could fog a mirror given control of a two-ton metal projectile and set loose on the public roads. The climber said that he felt safer on the mountain. I understood him now, having experienced the onrush of "too many variables." The paralyzing, uncontrollable too-muchness of the city.

My world had changed completely, every atom and particle transformed, but for everyone else it was business as usual. The day my father died, I had been stupefied to stagger out of the hospital and see that people were still walking around as if nothing had happened. They were chatting about banalities, wondering where to go for lunch, after he flatlined on the operating table during bypass surgery. At twelve, I could hardly believe the cruel indifference of others. Even my mother had been dry-eyed and subdued, as if the blow had landed outside her own body and I was the only one with unshielded feelings. The only one who could be seriously hurt.

Now Tim sometimes acted like I was hypersensitive, the sitcom version of an overprotective mother. He treated Charles like a new toy, a complicated one with as-yet-untested physical properties. How high could Charles be thrown, Tim appeared to wonder, before snatching his falling body from the air at the last second. If you strapped Charles to the back of your bike, how fast could you go? He had seen other babies fly by at fifteen miles an hour, their giant helmeted heads bobbing. Could Charles do that?

Meanwhile, I felt like my heart had been snapped into two jagged pieces like a girl's necklace. One half of the heart (*BEST*) remained inside my chest, while Charles (*FRIENDS*) was the still-beating other half, now horribly exposed.

"Will you calm down? He's not—"

"The strap is *loose*. It's hanging off him. Can't you see that? Wait, just let me—"

"Stop freaking out, Cara. He's fine. We're just going down the hall and back."

"Don't take him past the stairs like that. He's falling over!"

Tim continued to wheel Charles out the door, wide-eyed and listing in a plastic chair tied to Tim's neon bike. Some sporty coworker, for whom I felt a boiling hatred, had loaned Tim the infant bike seat after his toddler had outgrown it. But I did not want Charles strapped to a flimsy road bike, touring the city in the most crushable way, nor did I want Tim becoming an urban figure I instinctively distrusted: a Cool Dad.

Why couldn't he *listen* to me? It would be so easy, cost him so little. In difficult moments, I tried to recall what I'd seen in Tim: why *this* man, of all men on earth, when I was young and had barely dated at all? He had been nice-looking and smart, and we'd had fun, but it was more than that. Beneath all the snark and bravado, he had struck me as being orphaned. A young man alone in the world.

Through a scrim of ironic stories, I could picture Tim as a child: his brittle, well-to-do family erupting into acrimony and divorce; his dad marrying the girlfriend-on-the-side, resulting in a second son just as the first was unceremoniously shipped off to boarding school; his mother permanently enraged, a psychodrama in which Tim played a half-forgotten minor part. He had one job, to maintain the family's status and become a doctor, which he failed or refused to do, thus becoming his mother's second male letdown. Tim mentioned all of this offhandedly, as if it were a joke, but in my heart, some old, familiar pity stirred. My father, too, had seemed an orphan and a misfit, far from home. Grown-up and newly abandoned to the world for some purpose I did not know—possibly no purpose at all—I felt like an orphan myself. So, in affection and commiseration, I took up with Tim: two children bravely walking hand-in-hand into the woods.

All the males in my life—my father, Tim, and Charles—elicited feminine pity, a natural upswell over which I had no control. But now, to my alarm, I saw Tim had little pity for me. Ever since I—we—had decided I would not go back to work after my six-week maternity leave because it made little financial sense to put Charles in day care; ever since I had phoned Ben and given notice, feeling relieved and happy that I could stay home, Tim had been different, more distracted. His manner toward me had cooled. Once more, it was like he was trying to work through a difficult math problem in his mind, except, this time, *I* was the problem. I was the maddening *x*, the variable that couldn't be solved.

Maybe he was stressed about money. Always preoccupied with work, he seemed more conscious of his status there than ever. He rambled endlessly about the whims and demands of his editor, a mercurial father figure. Now the sole earner in the household, Tim was working hard, vying for a promotion and a much-needed raise. But on another, less rational level, he seemed to be chasing approval, pellets of validation he'd given up on getting from me. In fact, he seemed to feel I'd turned on him, somehow: no longer cheerful and supportive but needy, moody, and focused entirely on someone else.

As a result, Tim was not much inclined to listen to my worries. In his off-hours, he was determined to have fun with his son, a cool new toy his stay-at-home wife got to play with all the time. If I had a problem with that, Tim's back seemed to say as he ambled out the door, too bad for me.

I followed them into the hall and screamed at Tim's retreating form. Everyone heard the fight, no doubt—the Aesthete bowing his cello, the Angry Ballerina down the hall, maybe even the Missionaries and Tabitha, one floor down—but at that moment, I was beyond caring. Tim kept on rolling the bike slowly past the stairs and didn't look back. His head bent, he was now conversing one-sidedly with Charles, as if he'd found a new ally against hysterical females.

"I *forbid* you to take him out of the building, do hear me? He can't even sit up! Look at him. It isn't *safe*, it isn't—"

"Will you *shut up*? There's nothing to worry about. You're acting crazy!"

"No, I won't shut up! *You* shut up. You obviously have no idea what you're doing!"

I cannot overstate how tired we both were. After months of sleep deprivation, our brains were fried, zapped by every crackling jolt of feeling. We could not quite control our words or actions anymore. Something in us had slipped the leash and now roamed dangerously free.

Tim turned to look at me, one hand steadying the infant seat, and flipped me the bird.

WHAT KIND OF MOVIE WERE WE IN?

At first, it had been a rom-com: lighthearted, flirty, full of laughs, set to a bubbly pop soundtrack. When we moved to the city, the film changed into a buddy flick: coequal partners sharing a place, working, and chasing adventures. Now, the genre had changed again. Tim, Charles, and I were characters in a new story. Surely, it was a family movie, G-rated and uplifting: *The Swiss Family Robinson* or *The Sound of Music*, or maybe something cheesy and made-for-TV, a harmless tale of children, Santa Claus, and puppies.

But our lives did not feel like a family movie. Across the mildest scene—trips to the beach, or Charles arcing through the air in a baby swing—a shadow fell. Some underlying tension refused to resolve. It merely receded for a while before coming back, stronger.

Standing in the hall, barefoot, my hair unraveling from its knot, another movie category came to mind, one I had never liked. Horror had always struck me as fake, full of predictable conventions: jump-scares, uncanny lighting, ominous music, an eerie calm punctuated by spasms of violence, clothes drenched in blood, close-ups of women's screaming mouths. Back in the day, I had given horror short shrift. But ever since Charles was born, I'd understood the genre better. As an art form, it now struck me as important, even profound.

Horror, it turned out, was more real than I'd thought.

10

THE CITY'S SEASONS CHANGED, THEN CHANGED AGAIN. CHARLES turned one.

He now stood upright, one hand on the couch, grinning at me with bright new teeth. At times, hilarity overtook him, and he laughed so hard he fell down on his bottom with a thump.

"What exactly do you two do all day?" asked Tim.

"We are *flâneurs*," I said, stirring a pot. "We walk the city in order to experience it. We saunter, we loaf."

"I'm not familiar with that term."

"The French poet Baudelaire—could you pass me the salt? thanks—defined it as a gentleman stroller of the city streets. Charles is the gentleman stroller, technically the gentleman *in* the stroller, and I am his female caretaker. His *flâneuse*."

"Well, the next time you're out *flâneur*ing, could you pick up some hand soap and shampoo? Every time I'm in the bathroom, I find myself trying to bang the last drops out of an empty container."

"I'm sorry," I said. "I always forget things like that. I'll make a list."

"Don't you notice it, too?"

"I try not to go in there." A thin, sinuous crack was forming in the yellow tile between the sink's pedestal base and the wicker cabinet. Each time I saw it, it seemed longer and also, somehow, inevitable. The floor was shifting under our feet, rupturing in a hairline fracture. I tried to keep my gaze up, up, and pretend that I didn't notice.

In bed one night, we sat reading side by side: him an issue of *Scientific American*, me a faded book of poems by Baudelaire.

"*The Flowers of Evil*, huh?" Tim said dryly.

The French title was *Les Fleurs du Mal*, which sounded better, but before I could explain, Tim turned back to his magazine. He seemed to know less and less about me—my interests, my thoughts—like someone whose kite was slipping away into the sky and out of sight. I was the kite.

On my bedside table was another hardback: *Evil: An Investigation,* written by a journalist named Lance Morrow, though it was not so much journalism as a long, scattershot rumination. Its chapters circled around a series of propositions, telling stories, unpacking themes, hinting at depths. The subject was limned over and over:

"Evil has a wandering, fluid quality; it drifts like thought."

"Evil registers itself upon the deepest, most primitively feeling areas of the brain…"

"Evil plays with mirrors in order to confuse the mind…"

"Maybe evil is not an anomaly but the rule."

I felt a pressing need to ascertain the nature of reality, not as an academic matter, but because I had brought a child into it. If, per this journalist, evil was everywhere, what then was good?

Charles himself was good. Well, mostly. At any moment, I would have willingly laid down my life for Charles; he was the person I loved more than anyone else. Yet, even through him, there ran a thin vein of something else. A crooked thing I could not put my finger on.

AROUND THE TIME I BECAME OBSESSED WITH EVIL, I ALSO BECAME obsessed with getting new towels. Far down a wide commercial street sat a little shop that sold bath linens, and sometimes I would roll Charles's stroller inside and inspect the merchandise. Modern white shelves reached to the ceiling, filled with luxuriant rolls of 100% Egyptian cotton in jewel tones. I knew nothing of the global cotton hierarchy, but the shop's owner, an elderly Egyptian, assured me these were the world's finest towels, a statement I had no reason to question.

With his thick accent, lined brown face, and formal clothes, the old Egyptian seemed to be speaking of cotton as a trivial ruse, some kind of code, when what he really sought to impart was the gnomic wisdom of an ancient land. "Before using, wash and dry twice, but never on hot!" he admonished in a low voice gravelly with the residue of decades, of continents.

"Never on hot," I repeated.

"With every use, they will get softer. Low-quality towels become scratchy and stiff. But these *get softer*."

"Wow."

"Which color? You see here, we have all colors."

I studied the towers of towels. "Green, I think. That forest green." The fuzzy wedge reminded me of nature, some restorative place that was not the city waiting implacably for us in shades of gray and brick.

"Ah," the shop owner said, nodding. From somewhere behind the counter came the music of a flute-like instrument over strings. I glanced at Charles, strapped down with a chewable ring which now dangled between his feet. His eyes darted around the store, and he appeared on the verge of a scream.

"I need to talk to my husband," I said, sorry that I could not that minute drop two hundred dollars on towels, the towels that would usher in a better life. "I'd better get the baby home."

"Of course! This is your first child?"

"Yes. My only child. Though we may—well, we may be having another one."

"Ah! Very nice."

"I don't know how we're going to manage two," I remarked absently, wheeling the giant stroller around to the angle at which it would fit out the door.

"It's in God's hands."

"Yeah, I guess so. Well, see you later!"

"Only God can protect them." He had folded his hands and gazed at Charles.

"Bye!"

I HADN'T BEEN TRYING TO GET PREGNANT (WHICH, UNTIL TIM GOT A promotion, was not the plan), but I hadn't tried to prevent it, either. I'd always wanted more than one child, having been raised in a quiet house with no playmates. I didn't want that loneliness for Charles. Now some part of me sensed the need to have the second baby right away: to get it in under the wire before whatever was going to happen, happened.

I had not yet found a good time to inform Tim that our unplanned second child was on the way. Instead, I advocated passionately for home improvements. "None of our towels match, and there's a crack in the bathroom floor next to the sink. I'm here all day, and it's depressing. This place is beginning to fall apart!"

Tim said he'd left a message for Shelley, but she was not interested in our crack. He found a board somewhere and sawed it into a wooden mat with ragged edges. As I looked on, he placed the board over the crack and a small rug over the board.

"So, that's your solution. Are you kidding me?"

"That's the best I can do. I can't repair the floor. It's a historic building."

"Can't or won't?" I demanded waspishly. "You call yourself a reporter, and yet you can't even get our landlord to call us back! How do you function—"

"Cara."

"—at a major newspaper? Do I need to help you get a call returned?"

"You're getting worked up over nothing. It's just a little—"

"You don't care about it because you're never here! Charles and I and this whole place are just an afterthought."

"That's not fair. I don't go anywhere but the office and home. And maybe hit the gym once in a while. I can't remember the last time I did anything that would be remotely considered fun."

"Oh, thanks a lot!"

The following Saturday, Tim drove me down the street and waited in the car with Charles while I filled four bags with green towels. In his own way, he wanted to make me happy.

In fact, my moods were increasingly unpredictable and jagged. My daily stroller walks with Charles were growing longer, more ambitious. They veered off in impulsive directions, searching out soothing, secret pockets of the city.

The plastic playground by the lake made me nervous. There were too many adults, too many kids, too many dogs, too much of everything. An edgy atmosphere of forced gaiety prevailed, and all the parents looked exhausted. A clutch of nannies gossiped in Spanish on a bench while the children climbed and shrieked.

So, instead of heading to the playground, we often walked to a rose garden, tucked away off a main street. Wonderfully designed and landscaped, it was shaped like an amphitheater: a broad central walkway whose sides sloped up to higher ground. At the center of the walkway was a long reflecting pool in a tiled basin about two feet high, just tall enough for Charles to hang onto the edge. Surrounding the pool and up the sides were a series of paths lush with rose bushes of all colors and varieties. I sometimes read their English names to Charles in an impromptu poem: About Face, Carefree Beauty, Moody Blue, Oh My!

One late spring afternoon, we lingered by the pool as the sun beat down. Surrounding us, thousands of fragrant flowers bloomed. Cascading fountains built into the garden's sloping sides poured water from one rocky outcropping to the next. The hum of traffic a few blocks over was pierced by sirens, moving closer, then away and out of range. A handful of solitary figures milled about, backpack-laden students and retired people: reading, resting. I sat on the pool's cement edge, vaguely aware of Charles splashing its bright surface with his hand some feet away.

Up by a fountain, a girl was holding a baby in a blanket. Her long, dark hair was loose; her silver-gray dress caught the light. Even at a distance, I could see she was exceptionally pretty. I studied her. A college student, maybe? Now she was fussing with the blanket, lifting it from the baby's face and shifting her weight so that, instead of standing sideways, she turned slightly toward us. A moment passed, and she redraped the wrap over the child's head. This happened several more times: She uncovered the baby, covered it, paused, uncovered it again. She never looked up but seemed to perform with the awareness of an audience.

"Charles?" I looked around but didn't see him at my side.

I stood up and scanned the walkway. "Charles?"

Within seconds, I saw his face at the water's edge: Holding the rim, he'd toddled down the long side of the pool and around the corner, where he'd bent down to inspect something on the ground. I reached him in a few long strides and scooped him up.

"Where did you go?" I said. "I couldn't find you!"

I looked back up toward the girl, but she was gone. I searched the garden up and down, all the steps and paths leading out. How did she disappear so fast?

It suddenly seemed possible I had imagined her.

"I've discovered something interesting," Tim said.

"What's that?"

"You know how I always had sandwiches for lunch? Well, I've been going to this new place down the street—Jill turned me onto it—and they serve something called 'bone broth.' Basically, you take, say, a beef bone and simmer it with root vegetables—"

"That sounds like broth."

"Yes, but it's full of micronutrients. They serve it in a little cup. It's surprisingly filling. After that and a lettuce wrap, I have so much energy! It's amazing."

"Huh."

"We should start thinking about putting Charles on some version of a Paleo diet, adjusted for children of course. It's a more natural way of eating."

"I hope you're not going to get obsessed with food like everybody else. That's fine for people who have nothing else to talk about, but we—"

But Tim's expression had hardened and his tone changed. "Well, maybe you should be more obsessed with it. You have a child to feed, after all."

"Don't you think I know that? But Tim, trust me: What he eats is going to be the least of our problems. This is a healthy American child. The stores are bursting with good food. Let's give him a carrot and a gummy vitamin and shut up about it."

"Which, coincidentally, requires the least effort from you. Because you're so busy, right, Cara? Reading poems, going for walks."

"I'm thinking," I replied. "I'm caring for our son, and I'm thinking. And by the way, he's perfectly well-fed. The doctor said his weight is ideal. I'm just not boring both of us to death by talking about it."

"Oh, now I'm boring you to death? Just unbelievable."

"Yes, you are boring, if you want to know. You think the same things everyone else thinks. If someone were to pick you up and plunk you down two hundred years ago in a whole different country, you'd fall right into line, talking about the fishing boats and the best glogg. I don't know how I married somebody so *ordinary*."

"You're a stay-at-home mom!" Tim shouted. "What's more ordinary than that? What have you actually accomplished, besides quitting every job you've ever had?"

"I'm accomplishing it now. At least, I'm trying to accomplish it. We have one shot, Tim. How can you not see that? We have to get it right. I don't want him turning out like all these trendy, jaded people with meaningless lives—"

"Oh save it, Cara." Tim headed for the door. "Who died and made you Queen of Everything?"

LATER THAT DAY, I BURST INTO TEARS AND CONFESSED THAT I WAS pregnant.

Tim was sorry, I was sorry, we both were sorry. We had to do better.

Tim told me that he was concerned. I didn't seem well. He worried about us during the day. He wanted me to see a therapist on our plan.

I looked up at him through wet lashes, painfully aware things were happening that he could not understand. My very consciousness was changing, maybe from the latest wave of hormones crashing in, and all I could do was try to stay with him here, hanging on.

I'd go to therapy, attempt to tell the truth. But anyone with sense could see that I was not—maybe had never been—entirely reliable.

11

DAY 7

ONE WEEK DOWN AT MILDRED W. I MUST ADMIT, I FEEL CALMER.
Probably because, in addition to the SSRI that takes a while to kick in,
they gave me a pill to help me sleep.

Now, despite the narrow bed, the crackling pillowcase, the one-star
thread count, and the 24/7 hallway light that creeps under the door,
I'm sleeping better than I have in years. I barely dreamed at home,
subconsciously primed for a baby's cry. But here, I sink luxuriously
into dreams like movies: vivid stories with surprise plot twists and
striking effects. Like movies, they seem more intense than real life, rich
with emotions inexpressible in waking hours. Every morning, I wake
up blinking and reluctantly rejoin the world, like someone stepping
into the bright, hard light of day after a show.

A WEEK AGO, I WASN'T IN GREAT SHAPE. WHY DIDN'T I REALIZE SOONER
that I needed help? Why didn't Tim? I was so used to feeling anxious
and overwhelmed, running on fumes, that this unstable state of mind
seemed normal, hardly worth mentioning. Dashing around between
work calls and family outings designed to check the "quality time"
box, Tim gave no outward sign that anything was wrong; his manner
was matter-of-fact verging on annoyed. I was a functionary who was
glitching out, my performance dipping into the suboptimal. Could I
please just get it together?

So, when they brought me in, I felt embarrassed by all the attention.
I tucked my chin and mumbled through the intake interview like
someone cornered at a party and peppered with personal questions.
If the conversation was recorded—it may have been for all I know—a
portion of the transcript would go like this:

A: It doesn't matter. I'm not going to do anything. I need to
get home.

Q: Why are you so sure you're not going to do anything, as you put it? You appear troubled, you're not sleeping. You've spoken of recurrent thoughts—

A: Because I have two kids to raise. They're very young. It's not like I have an option. There's no one else.

Q: What about your husband? He seems very concerned for you and the children.

A: No, Tim can't do it.

Q: He can't do what?

A: He thinks he can, but it won't be enough. He won't know what he's doing. They'll grow up [inaudible].

Q: Could you repeat that, please? I didn't get the last word.

A: Lost. They'll grow up lost.

Q: And do you feel lost?

A: Well, I'm in here, aren't I. [inaudible]

Q: Here. Have a tissue.

A: [inaudible]

Q: Are you okay?

A: [inaudible]

Q: Mrs. Nielsen?

A: Sorry. I have to get home. How long before I can go home?

Q: That depends.

For several moments, I said nothing. Part of me didn't want to know on what, exactly, it depended.

I'M GETTING ACCUSTOMED TO THE DAY'S SLOW RHYTHMS: BREAKFAST, art therapy, lunch, group, quiet time, dinner, evening rec. Not everyone is allowed in the Rec Room, but that's what makes it nice: a café atmosphere of low couches and tables, the central island of the nurses' station, people reading or chatting or in a quiet funk of rumination. It lacks coffee, but everyone's mood is finely calibrated to be stable: A vente latte or caramel-whip-topped sugar bomb might throw someone off, causing them to be promptly escorted from the Rec Room, which would be too bad. Steady as she goes.

Last night I was sitting on one half of an orange couch, gathering my thoughts, when a girl of about nineteen sat down next to me. She had short dark hair and a multiracial face, an unusual face. After some minutes of silence, she introduced herself. "I'm Flee."

"Flea?" I said.

"Two Es. As in, *go*. Flee."

"Oh. Okay. I'm Cara."

"Makes you do things."

"Sorry?"

"Don't want to."

I said nothing.

"Makes you, makes you," sang Flee. After a moment, she added, "Don't you agree?"

"I'm sorry. I didn't quite hear you."

She turned her face to me and seemed to take me in, all at a glance. Whatever she was, she was not stupid. I'd never seen a person suffer fools less gladly.

Hands loose and slightly crumpled, she raised her forearms to her face. "The Devil makes you do things you don't want to do."

I saw her arms had been slashed over and over. A dozen thin lines, healed pink.

I nodded, and we sat in silence for a while. "I'm just going to…" I began, hoping to make an exit without being rude.

"You think you don't belong here." It was not an accusation, just a statement of fact.

"Well, I—"

"I didn't think so either, my first time. Guess what number this is."

"I don't know. Three?"

"No. Lucky seven. It always feels safe in here. Boring but safe. It's frightening out there, you know?"

"Yes. I know," I said. "The city scares me sometimes, too."

"The Devil—" she began.

"I don't really believe in that," I mumbled.

"Oh? What's it for you, then?"

"What's what?"

"What *do* you believe in that scares you?"

"It doesn't have a name," I said. "It's like a mist or a…force field, you can feel it sometimes. It's very dark. That's all I know."

Flee took this in. "Like where?" she asked.

"Oh, I don't know. Everywhere."

"…Yeah."

12

OUR DAUGHTER BEATRICE WAS NAMED AFTER THE HEROINE OF A PLAY. Back in college, when I spent my days mulling phrases on a grassy slope, I was struck by something she said—Shakespeare's Beatrice, that is. She tossed it off at a party, just repartee. Someone remarks to Beatrice, who's being uncharacteristically quiet, that merriness "best becomes you, for out o' question you were born in a merry hour."

Beatrice replies, "No, sure, my lord, my mother cried, but then there was a star danced, and under that I was born."

My mother cried, but then there was a star danced... This seemed a brilliant young person's attempt to get out from under the pain of womanhood—the weight of it, the blood and tears—and to claim for herself another birthright, all light and space and freedom. *My mother was a wreck, but I'm not like her; nothing can stop me*, she says. That "but"—so pitiless, so quick to abandon.

I'm not like other girls. At one time, I had worn this statement as a badge of honor. It seemed to make me special, more attractive— certainly to Tim. But I had been young and naïve, undifferentiated as an egg. I was beginning to suspect I was a lot like other girls, distinctly female, no matter how inconvenient anyone found it.

Now I had my own Beatrice, my own fresh scar. Was she born in a merry hour? I hoped she was.

So far, she was a prim and serious little thing. It stunned me to see her, all of nine pounds, pull herself together after some diarrheal explosion or nostril irrigation or other monstrous indignity. She seemed to try not to make trouble while her brother like a small Hannibal pressed on in his devastating campaign: toppling lamps, emptying cupboards, yanking the cat's feathery tail.

Charles, too, had been a good baby, with the contentment of an emperor who assumes the world exists for his pleasure and conquest. But Bea at six weeks seemed to understand that much would be asked of her. There was a strain of can-do women in our family, and though I didn't feel like one myself, it seemed entirely possible she would be one of them. People said she looked like me, but to me she looked like only herself: an as-yet-mysterious being, playing her cards close to the vest.

Tucked in a pouch around my chest, she moved with me throughout the day: a sidekick, treasure, spirit animal. I found her excellent company.

AT MY PRENATAL APPOINTMENTS, TIM HAD PEPPERED THE DOCTOR with multi-part queries like an ace reporter at a White House briefing, making me want to cuff him from where I sat half-naked in a paper dress. Many of his questions had concerned whether our second child's birth via C-section would involve Dr. Rodd.

Rodd was the anesthesiologist who'd been on call during the harrowing extraction of Charles. In a soothing baritone, he had talked me through the epidural and pre-surgical prep, giving me to understand that being sliced open under emergency conditions while fully conscious would be a piece of cake: At most, I would feel "a little tug." Afterward, my immense relief at having a healthy baby and generous supply of painkilling drugs fixed on Rodd, and when he came around to see how I was doing, I nearly blew him kisses.

For one wild, tear-streaked moment, he had been my favorite person in the world. But by now, I was pretty much over him. It all seemed long ago, and in the process of scheduling my second C-section, which mostly consisted of filling out paperwork that legally absolved the hospital in the event of my death, I figured anyone could dope me up and probably get it right. The doctors were matter-of-fact, upbeat about a simple slash-and-grab. I felt cautiously optimistic. The important thing, we all agreed, was that when all was said and done, I would be no longer be pregnant. Cheers!

In the matter of Dr. Rodd, however, Tim was adamant. Would he be working on our scheduled date? When would my doctor know about his schedule? Was he usually "on" mornings or nights? Should we wait to choose a date until we knew for certain he would be there? Any chance he'd be on vacation that week? Because we could wait!

My doctor, a young Asian woman in metal-rimmed glasses, seemed perplexed. Compared to other dads, Tim probably seemed a freak of paternal involvement, a Grand Inquisitor of obstetric procedure who could knowledgeably talk about Braxton-Hicks and dosages down to the cc. Was he some kind of trial lawyer? Would he just let her do her job?

"Is there," she said carefully, "some specific reason you'd like Dr. Rodd?"

Tim explained that he'd been great last time, and it would really mean a lot to me to know he was there again. To make sure the pain was, you know, dealt with.

The doctor looked at me. Raising one eyebrow a barely perceptible degree, I indicated that my husband, while well-meaning, was a little nuts on this subject. With an infinitesimal quiver of her chin, she indicated she understood perfectly.

"Well," she said in a reassuring tone to Tim, "because you're scheduled for a weekday morning, there's a very good chance that Dr. Rodd will be the attending physician. But I'll be happy to look into it and get back to you."

"That would be great! Thanks so much."

"Any other questions?"

"No," we both said.

"Then I'll see you next time."

Tim rose to leave. "Thanks, Dr. Hua. We really appreciate it."

"Let me just—" I murmured. "My clothes."

"Right." He sat down again.

"Take care," said Dr. Hua.

After a few more rounds of this back-and-forth, I began to suspect Tim had his own reasons for wanting Dr. Rodd to administer the drip. Consciously, perhaps, it was as he said: Rodd was a rock star, as we knew from experience. Only the best for the little lady! But was it really about me? Rodd was tall and fair with a deep, sonorous voice. He seemed larger-than-life, like a bigger version of Tim, with something of Tim's prep school looks and subtle air of noblesse oblige. On some level, I sensed, Tim felt that having Rodd's manly and capable presence at the helm would make up for his own wavering interest in my life and health, my sobs and fears, my unceasing maternal drama. This pregnancy had strung me out like an addict on hormonal junk—weeping, crazed, blinking with scorched eyes, unable to discern reality from shadow. Maybe Tim felt that Rodd and only Rodd could deal with me at this point. Leave it to Rodd! Tim had had enough.

At 5 a.m. on delivery morning, I applied my makeup, gazing steadily into my own eyes in the gray-white bathroom light. I felt like a warrior heading into battle in full paint. As Crazy Horse said, it was a good day to die. It was a good day to give birth, or to die while giving birth, or whatever would happen. My lipstick was a rosy nude. Red would have been better, but it was too late now.

Set to remain at home with Charles, Claudia seemed nervous about my impending date with some faceless surgeon. By dawn, she had wiped down the counters and seemed at the end of her resources. Meanwhile, I was cracking jokes, finding the situation suddenly hilarious. "Is she on something?" Claudia asked Tim.

"No, that's all her."

"I feel great!" I said, buzzing with nervous energy. "I'm really taking a bullet for the team here. I want you guys to remember that." Now Claudia looked mildly alarmed. "Don't worry, Mom! Everything will be fine."

"I'll call you later," Tim told her, bundling me out the door.

Flat on my back in the white light of the O.R., I sobered up. Events as they were unfolding seemed to lack poetry, somehow. Perhaps they lacked actual poetry. Should Tim be reading me a poem? Should we be clutching hands and praying? There didn't seem enough to do. Should we have music on? We were having a child! Why did it seem so blandly medical, like a glorified trip to the dentist?

Tim was holding my hand but seemed enthralled by the presence of Dr. Rodd. As the nurses busied themselves draping me and readying their tools, Tim said to Rodd, who was standing just out of sight behind my head, "So, what do you drive?"

These words, building on some earlier strand of small talk, stunned me to my core. What on earth was going on? Were my husband and Dr. Rodd going to talk about *cars*? For an eternal thirty seconds, they compared models. The surgery began. It seemed impossible to tell Tim to be quiet. We were so physically close to the people operating on me, it would have been rude. What kind of woman carps at her husband in the middle of a C-section?

Tim was enthusing over Dr. Rodd's mileage. I closed my eyes. It was all going to be fine. It was a good day to be born. Just a little bit longer... Taking a deep breath, I gave Tim's hand a hard squeeze. He seemed to recall where he was, said something reassuring. But it was too late: I would take this betrayal to my grave. We should have read a poem for her. It was her big day, and we flubbed it. We were inadequate to the task of being parents. Why had nobody told us what to do? *I'm sorry. I'm sorry.*

With a lusty wail, Beatrice arrived. We knew she was coming and here she was, sticking the landing like a champ. A girl, finally. A girl. Good.

I was tired of men.

"So you gave the cat away," said Gemma three weeks later.

"We didn't give her away," I said. "We sort of boarded her."

"You boarded her with the Old Woman."

"We call her Tabitha now. Yes."

"Because Charles was getting into the litter box. Right?"

"Right. You can't have a toddler and a litter box in a one-bedroom apartment. It's just crazy. Before the baby, I could swoop it out of his way because I followed him everywhere. But now I have to let him out of my sight sometimes."

"But, so... When do you think you'll be able to take Mew back?"

"When we get a bigger place. Ha. Or when Charles is older. Maybe in two years, when he's four."

"But then won't Bea be two?"

"I don't know, Gemma. I'm just trying to survive right now. Mew is better off there, believe me. Tabitha dotes on her all day. She combs her, brushes her *teeth*. I hardly even brush my own teeth."

We were in a leather-and-mahogany steakhouse bar. The din of happy hour noise required us to yell a little, but it all seemed glamorous to me: the blood-red cloth napkins, the cubes of crystal ice. Outside the floor-to-ceiling windows, the elements of a dazzling sunset were moving into place over the water, like showgirls hitting their marks in a grand finale.

Gemma looked good. She had grown out her hair, styled in what I believed was called a blowout. Her once-chewed fingernails were now wine-dark, high gloss. A diamond tennis bracelet—a present from her new boyfriend, Vivek—dangled from her wrist. He was a software developer who'd sold some shares and bought a four-bedroom house, which he shared with roommates. Gemma had quit her job as a copy editor and now did marketing for his company.

"Ben's sweet," she said, "but that place was so boring. I don't know how I stuck it out so long. Next month, we're all flying to Singapore. First class!"

"That sounds incredible! Good for you. I'm glad you're happy." I gave what I hoped was an encouraging smile, but some part of me felt betrayed or left behind by the new Gemma. We had started out so alike, two bored girls in adjacent cubicles on the seventh floor of a nondescript office building, happy to fling ourselves into the streets together every day. But now the road had forked into a Y, and every step took us further apart. Gemma's life seemed pointless and tiring to me: an endless loop of restaurants, marketing, shopping, and travel. But I had reason to suspect that my life didn't seem great to her, either.

"So, how are things with Tim?" she asked, popping a bite of sesame-flecked seared tuna into her mouth.

"It's hard to say." I paused, unsure how much I could explain to Gemma, aglow from landing a high-earning superboyfriend. Tim and I were still an affectionate couple, intermittently. But qualities I once admired in him—his sharp, logical mind and dedication to his work—now seemed beside the point if not actively irritating. He seemed unable to grasp what was right in front of him: Our lives had changed. There was no going back to our first years in the city, when we spent Friday nights talking shop over ceviche, a house-smoked charcuterie board, or the pool table of a hipster dive bar. Everything was different now. I was different.

Tim didn't seem to like me very much this way. It was as if I'd broken some unspoken pact to be buddies, colleagues, and co-earners; like this whole mom-with-baby thing was some outrageous bait-and-switch. And to be fair, he had a point: It was a switch. Now with a toddler and a newborn, I had no need for a roomie or a playmate. Instead, I needed someone to *provide*—that quaint, charged word—financial cover and logistical backup for me and the children, who clearly needed me at home during these, their infant years. Tim acted like all this was a bolt from the blue, like his old girlfriend had been body-snatched by a teary, demanding wraith he wouldn't have dated for a month. Maybe I was being unfair, attempting to rewrite the terms of our marriage. I didn't know if it was fair; I just knew how I felt.

"When I was pregnant with Bea, he kept asking when I was going back to work, what was the 'plan.' I said, 'Could you just let me have this baby? I'm kind of busy here.' Meanwhile Charles is crawling all over me, the apartment's a mess. He didn't act like any of it was his problem. He seemed to feel that I wasn't doing *enough*."

"Wow," said Gemma. She took a long sip of her drink, settling in for a chilling tale of The Horrors of Married Life.

"We fought so much when I was pregnant. It wasn't good. We turned into one of those couples arguing in public, in full view of strangers. I picked up Charles and walked out of a donut shop once, Tim was making me so crazy."

"What did he do?"

"For one, embarrassed me in front of this old man. The three of us were in a booth, and this old guy, maybe eighty, was sitting in the next booth over. I was saying to Tim that, eventually, I'd like to go back to work part time. Then Tim goes, 'Well, if you get to work part time, then I should get to work part time.' Like it's some game where everything has to balance out. Not that he'd ever switch to part time, he was just arguing on principle. I said, 'Well, someone has to work full time while I take care of the kids.' And Tim says, 'Hey, they're my kids too!' He gave me zero credit for being the mom, the one who's breastfeeding and carrying them around ten hours a day. He wanted everything exactly equal so he didn't have to feel burdened with supporting us. Meanwhile, I'm aware that this old guy can hear our conversation and can also see that I'm hugely pregnant, with a toddler. And I'm thinking to myself, 'To this old guy, Tim must sound like a real jerk.' So after a few choice words, I picked up Charles and waddled out."

"Hmm. So, did you also think he was being a jerk?" Her brow furrowed with the effort to empathize with my plight, which, every time she saw me, seemed to be getting worse.

I paused to consider this question, chin in my hand. For long seconds I cast about for some principle to hang my hat on. Finally, I said, "I understand that every family is different. It's not the 1950s anymore. There are a lot of ways to handle things. Do I think the old-fashioned way is the only or best way? Not necessarily. It all depends. I'd never judge anyone for their choices. But in our particular case? Yes, I thought Tim was being a huge jerk."

"Ugh," Gemma said. "It's really tricky." She seemed unsure whose side to take, and I couldn't blame her. Maybe the whole thing was, on some level, my fault. How hard was it to find a rich guy in the city? What did I expect, marrying a newspaper reporter?

"I'm sure we'll figure something out. He's home with both kids right now. God knows how he's managing. It's weird being away from Bea. It feels like I should be rocking, not just sitting."

"Did you want dessert, Cara?" Gemma asked after a pause. "Have something. It's on me."

"Mom?"

"Yes, Charles?" I was rocking in my chair, the baby curled to my chest.

"Mom?"

"Yes, sweetie?"

"Mom?"

"What is it, Charles?"

"Mama?"

"Yes, precious?"

"Mom?" I closed my eyes briefly. The baby stirred and whimpered almost inaudibly. Charles was gamboling around with a spatula in his hand, looking for action. It was about three o'clock on a weekday afternoon.

Beatrice opened her eyes, hazel-gray, and gazed up at me from my lap. Small and bright, they did not want to be blue. They wanted to be brown. I said, "How's the bunch?"

"Mom?" Charles queried. I ignored him.

"How's the bunchkin?" I pressed. "How's the munchkin bunchkin?" Bea wrinkled her nose and squinched her eyes like an old woman trapped on a city bus full of riffraff. "How's the munchkinny bunchkinny? How's the baby bunch?"

"Mom?" Charles asked uncertainly.

"What is it, Charles? How's the bunchess? How's the Bunchess of Bunchestire?"

"Mom?"

"How's Fraulein Bunchenhausen? How's Señorita Bunchita?"

"Mom?"

"Is the bunchkin sad? Is the munchkin bunchkin—*Charles*!"

A Bach adagio was playing in the background, as I had begun listening to Baroque choral arrangements. It was not to enhance my babies' intelligence, since Charles was already exhibiting a level of cunning that would serve him well at the highest echelons of law or finance. It was to enhance my own intelligence.

"Do you have a poo?" I asked. "Does the bunchkin have a poo?"

"Poo!"

"Charles, do *you* have a poo?"

"No."

"Are you sure?"

Silence.

"Charles?"

"Mom?"

"Yes?"

"…Phone?"

"I don't have a phone, Charles."

"Phone?"

"Where's *your* phone?"

"Phone?"

"Where's your Elmo phone? Does the bunchkin have a poo?"

"Mom?"

"Does the bunchkin have a stinky bottom? Let's check."

"Mom?"

"Nope! No poo. What's the matter? Does the bunchkin want a snicky snack?"

"Mom?"

"Charles, put that *down*! Put it *down*! Thank you. Look in your toy box for your Elmo phone."

"Coo?"

"You just had a cookie, Charles."

"Coo?"

"No, you just had one. Is the bunchkin hungry?"

"Mom?"

"Yes, Charles?"

"Mom?"

"Yes, sweetie?"

"Mom?"

This went on for ten more minutes before some Charles-precipitated crisis brought it to an abrupt end.

13

AT TWO YEARS OLD, CHARLES WAS THE MOST BEAUTIFUL PERSON I HAD ever seen. He was to me a wonder, a walking sublimity, whom I could hardly believe lived with us in our grubby apartment. He had fine golden hair, long-lashed blue eyes, and strawberry lips. His form was sturdy and long-limbed; his smile was wide, exuberant, dazzling. I would have happily spent hours cuddling this perfect creature, so unaccountably produced by me, but it was not to be.

Because Charles during this time was very bad. He wheedled, screamed, and disobeyed as if moved by some elemental force. One minute laughing at some bit of drollery from Elmo, the next could find him shocked and enraged that he was not allowed to climb into the dishwasher to play with dirty knives. He cried when thwarted in his aims to pillage our home, to menace the baby. He yelled and fussed for foods that no one could identify, for playtime at the park and at playtime's inevitable end, for a change of song on the stereo, for a binky he'd literally thrown into the sea.

By 9:30 a.m., I was tired of Charles. He was three hours into his day and had delighted and wearied me many times, with many more to go as we rowed toward the distant shores of naptime. It seemed impossible that I would spend my day in thrall to the passing manias of an infant. There had been some error; any moment now, reinforcements would arrive. The cavalry was coming—hold on!

But as I gazed around the wrecked and empty rooms, there was only Beatrice, regarding me owlishly from her basket. Meanwhile Charles had put some deadly object in his mouth, chewing and rolling it around in a careless way (*will he swallow it? should I call 911?*) before spitting it in a primordial wad of matter and saliva into my outstretched palm, flashing a movie star smile, and running off.

And the apartment! What had been a pleasant home for Tim, me, and the cat was now a cramped menagerie of beings indifferent to their bodily functions. I was obsessed with the movement of human waste in and out of the rooms: the scrubbing and airing of the diaper pail, the emptying of the kitchen trash in which a soiled onesie lurked amid the coffee grounds and Similac cartons. It was crucial to get this stuff (technically, this *crap*) out of the house because it stank, and more was coming, so we had to make room for it.

As an undergraduate studying the mystical poems of W.B. Yeats, I had been puzzled by a line in "Crazy Jane Talks with the Bishop":

Love has pitched his mansion
In the place of excrement.

But now I understood it perfectly. Jane was talking about our bedroom, where a mound of laundry hulked next to a reeking diaper bucket, where the marital sheets spent much time crushed and peed-on somewhere near the footboard. Our babies slept tangled between us; we lived among them wholly, deeply.

Truly, back then I had no idea this would be my life.

"I'm thinking I need to get out of here," I said.

"What?" Tim was in the kitchen making eggs while I slumped at the table next to our farmer's market gear: a metal-frame backpack made to carry a toddler, water bottles, bags. He looked around the corner with a dish towel boyishly flung over one shoulder.

"What if I went home for a while? Took the kids back to see my mom?"

"She was just out here for the birth."

"That was four months ago. And I could use a change of scene." In fact, my mother's house now seemed an ancestral palace, impressively vast and decked out with barely remembered luxuries. A comfortable couch flanked with armchairs, a dedicated laundry room, a kitchen outfitted with up-to-date silver appliances instead of cheap white rental junk, a front yard, a backyard, a wrought-iron patio table on the porch. A private garage where you could store your bike without a chain and bike lock. I had taken it all for granted, this normal life of things and space, blithely assuming Tim and I could recreate it somehow. Now I felt the need to go back, if only to recall something about myself, that erstwhile promising young girl who didn't spend her days in three cramped upstairs rooms.

"Teak," Charles uttered from his chair, shooting a leg out.

"Don't kick, Charles. What do you think?" I asked Tim.

"You think you could manage the kids? We've never flown with both of them."

"Teak!"

"No kicking, Charles," I repeated. "How hard can it be? Bea will probably sleep the whole time."

"It's fine with me. I'd come too, but I have that conference."

"The bioengineering thing? We could all go together when it's over."

"Teak!"

"There's always follow-up to do," Tim said, shutting down my suggestion. "It's swarming with national press, very competitive. But you guys should go, if you want. How long would you be gone?"

"Maybe a week."

"How are you doing, anyway? Are you basically okay, or—" Tim began.

"Teak!"

"*Charles, stop kicking the table!*" bellowed Tim. "Hey! Don't cry. It's okay."

"Charles, it's okay. Daddy isn't mad at you. Do you want to get down?"

"He's not done eating."

"Well, he's not going to eat now," I said to Tim. I released Charles from his chair and said to him, "Go find your Elmo."

"I know what you're doing," Tim said as Charles toddled away.

"*What?*" I snapped.

"You're trying to get away from Elmo."

"…Wow. You saw right through me," I replied, picking up on the joke.

"You want to fly away and leave Elmo with me! But I am sick of that guy's schtick."

"His little, furry, bright-red—"

"High-pitched Muppet schtick. No way he's staying with me."

"Able was I ere I saw Elmo," I quipped. "You know, the palindrome? About Napoleon?"

When Tim laughed, he looked like a grown version of Charles. It seemed good that we could still crack each other up.

IN THE DUSTY BLIP OF A TOWN WHERE I'D GROWN UP, LITTLE HAD changed. It was spring, when great flocks of birds rose in a cloud over the prairie, dipping and circling in synchronicity, a waking dream. Wind shook the bare-limbed trees and blew dirt in our eyes. We spent long days kicking a ball around the park, playing with Play-Doh, watching bulldozers at a construction site, and taking recreational trips to the car wash.

Away from the city and its complicated gauntlet of pre-K enrichment, I had to riff on basic features of the landscape. Driving through endless golden plains, Charles sightseeing from his car seat, I was forced to confront the flimflam in my head that passed for worldly knowledge.

"Cow!"

"That's not a cow, Charles. That's a horse. A horse is like a cow, but different." How was a horse not like a cow? I thought and thought. "They have different-shaped heads."

Several minutes passed.

Charles said, "Tane!"

On tracks parallel to the road, emerging weirdly from an infinite horizon like something out of Dali, chugged a fantastically complicated piece of yellow machinery. Three cars long and unmanned, it was perhaps a train-fixer. Or track-fixer.

"That's right, Charles. A train," I said. "A train with a… thing on it." He took this in. "It's yellow!"

As a teenager, I had longed to flee this mind-bending expanse, these swaths of farmland on which not a single bright word had been spoken. The sun baked the dirt and the vast clouds unfurled mutely. The prairie lightning was pre-verbal; the rains were tongue-tied; the trillion stars were dumb.

But now, I almost wished we could stay longer. Bad things happened in small towns, but they happened further apart—across fields and yards, across rutted back roads that saw no cars for days. The air seemed fresh, not clogged with pain and poison like the city's. Crimes and tragedies still occurred, but they somehow seemed more palatable here. The sun beat wordlessly down on the dirt. The vast clouds unfurled in the sky...

IT WAS IN THIS TOWN THAT I'D LEARNED TO LOVE THE MOVIES. MOVIES and books: my tickets out, on trains departing every hour from our sunken den. During my teen years, Claudia and I had shared the house like roommates, coming and going from work and school, setting up camps in different rooms. She liked to provide me with food and then withdraw discreetly, like a butler.

Now she treated me like a teenager who'd returned from distant lands, encumbered with a bulging diaper bag and two children. The kids were like my siblings here: younger and more interesting than me, full of potential. Meanwhile, back in my old room, I felt myself regressing to a pre-mother, pre-wife state. A moody teenager surrounded by nice stuff, touchy about something she couldn't put her finger on.

"Can I make you anything, Cara?" Claudia asked as I sat studiously doing nothing. "Grilled cheese?"

"That would be great."

"Do you want a pickle?"

"Yes, thanks."

"Ruffles or Lays?"

"Lays.

It seemed difficult to move to the kitchen, as if the couch were magnetized and I were a metal filling with no human agency. Claudia brought out a tray, took Bea from my arms, and arranged her on her lap. The three of us settled in to watch cable TV, which Tim and I had not had in years.

Within seconds, it was clear Claudia spent a lot of time in front of the television: a big, boxy model encased in a wall-sized cabinet that suddenly struck me as expensive. She scrolled through five hundred channels with an air of impatient familiarity. "Oh, this is good," she said. "Have you seen this?" It was a show about true crime.

In this episode, an adulteress hired a halfwit to bludgeon her husband. The job was botched. All her relatives and half the town looked on, grimly nodding, as, in heavy eyeliner, she received her twenty-five to life. Munching my sandwich, I longed to reflect on these events, but the show was already on to the next crime. Neglected teens shot their own grandparents and, out of spite, burned down their barns. Men strangled their neighbors with wire over disputes about a pasture fence. Grudges were nursed, children abandoned, warm corpses doused with kerosene. All over wounded feelings or—drum roll—"the insurance."

"How can you watch this stuff?" I said after an hour.

"It's kind of interesting," my mother said mildly, looking on with a practiced eye as EMTs removed an overweight dead body from a rusty trailer. The baby jounced on her lap, absorbed in the changing patterns on the screen. The old sensation of being feet away from Claudia, but somehow distant and alone, kicked in. She was semi-retired now, with a reduced teaching load and rare committee meetings in the afternoons. What did she do here all day, rattling around the ancestral palace like a distracted ghost, leafing through books, putting them down, beginning projects and abandoning them, and finally clicking on the TV? The sense that Claudia was somehow here but not here— after I'd traveled all this way!—suddenly irritated me.

"It's so depressing," I said flatly. "By the time it goes to commercial, I'm depressed."

"I don't find it depressing," Claudia said. The county coroner was explaining something about discoloration. "I just like to watch it because it's real."

"You mean instead of all the made-up murder shows? Those are horrible too, but at least they're fake."

"Well, I don't know," my mother said as a prosecutor pressed a seemingly obscure point about someone's underpants. "I guess I just can't believe how people behave."

"They behave badly," I informed her, hearing my own voice at fourteen.

The next day, I found her changing a gag-inducing diaper while, on TV, some self-styled stylist harangued a woman about her eyebrows. "Shouldn't you be watching America's Seediest Miscreants?" I asked. The baby turned my way and smiled uncertainly, as if trying to place me.

"Shouldn't you be watching America's Most Irredeemable Louts?" My mother silently mopped up my child with a seventeenth wipe.

"Shouldn't you be watching When Ex-Wives Attack?"

Eighteenth.

"Shouldn't you be watching—"

"Keep it up," Claudia said equably, "and I'll turn it on."

I slunk off to find Charles, peaceably disemboweling a potted plant. I loved that kid.

LATER THAT DAY, I FOUND MYSELF IN CLAUDIA'S OFFICE AT THE END OF the hall, past the linen closet, a large room that had once been part of the garage. An oak desk cluttered with papers and journals sat in its center, surrounded by two full bookshelves, a stereo, and a small TV. A nubby cardigan lay draped over a wheeled chair, which was pushed back from the giant desk as if Claudia had left it moments ago, interrupted by my arrival.

This was the human center of the house, the room most electric with presence, and standing in it felt oddly like being inside Claudia's mind. A studied disorder prevailed, suggesting an active dislike or distrust of order. Magazines, CD cases, and glasses half-filled with water cluttered the desk. Years-old syllabi and expired utility bills were thumbtacked to an ancient corkboard. As a child I had felt shy and out-of-place here, but now I cast an assessing gaze as if I were the anthropologist, gathering facts about an elusive tribe of one.

Claudia had always been productive in this setting, as if chaos soothed her. On the walls hung the totems and handicrafts of many lands, two framed diplomas, and a few yellowing pieces of school art from my childhood. Claudia studied the belief systems of various far-flung cultures: stories invented to explain or appease the confounding forces that ruled people's lives. A trained ethnologist, she cataloged beliefs, but in her considered view, it all seemed to amount to a lot of interesting nonsense.

Still, it was voluminously documented, and it kept her busy. I ran my index finger down the dusty surface of her desk, studying the objects arrayed before her when she sat there. A Mason jar with something sticky at the bottom, full of pens. A dog-eared campus directory and two legal pads. A framed photograph of my father, looking impossibly young in a cap and gown. A photograph of me in second grade, missing two teeth. A folded map, a reminder to schedule her six-month dental checkup, a small jade elephant, a mug bearing the logo of an academic conference nine years back. And framed in gold, the iconic, decades-old image of my brother as a toddler, laughing.

In a vanished world of bobby socks and Easter dresses, Claudia had been raised by blue-collar Polish Catholics. But by her college graduation, to hear her tell it, she had shrugged off most of her upbringing without a second thought. The known bored her. Only the exotic piqued her interest; hence her Ph.D. in anthropology and marriage to my foreign-born father.

For all this, in middle age, her life seemed rather dull, governed by the conventions of faculty life, with its departmental politics and abstruse squabbles. Nothing and no one in that world could explain what dark powers had swirled around a jetlagged young mother, years ago, causing her to go to the balcony and stretch her arms over the edge, offering up her baby as if in a trance. It was unthinkable, unreal. It couldn't happen so, officially, it hadn't.

Half-buried among the ephemera of her office was a small wooden figure in a beard and robe. I picked it up: some kind of carving of a saint, hands clasped in prayer and eyes downcast. It was a wee anonymous saint, like a gnome lurking in a garden. I turned it upside down, hoping to find a name or date etched into it. But the wooden statue offered no clue as to itself, signified nothing. I put it down next to a shiny black clay bowl and left the room.

It was funny about the birds. I thought of telling Tim, then decided against it.

I was walking in the field behind our house. Charles and Bea were down for naps, and I had stepped out for some air. The field stretched before me, scraggly with tough plants, weeds and thistles. Clouds filled the giant dome of sky, a rococo of pale grays and golds.

I'd always liked to watch the birds, as I never understood how they did it: rising and swelling in formation, a three-dimensional shape dancing across the sky. Scientists had penned the reasons, but no arrangement of words could explain it. Whatever the birds were doing in the high, clear air above our heads was unintelligible; no one could, in any real way, comprehend it.

Now, hundreds of dark starlings rose off a distant field like steam. All veered to the left, then the right, as if someone had flipped a switch. The shapes they formed had contours and depth: a paisley, an elongated sphere, a funnel, a heart. Back-and-forth over the prairie they flew, perhaps a half-mile from where I stood. And then, a distinct object took shape in the sky.

It was an ovoid form with two blank spaces near the top. A third space opened up below. A narrow column ran down the middle. In half a second, the shape flickered into being, holding its form as hundreds of starlings flew left to right, right to left.

"It's a face," I remarked to no one.

Was it a face? I blinked as it turned back into a flock, dipping and soaring.

Moments later, it reappeared with shocking clarity. A face made of wings hung in the sky, a semaphore of birds. When it dissolved, the starlings landed like a single curtain falling.

Shaken, I walked back into the house. Claudia was folding laundry, the children sleeping. Stretched out together on one bed, they looked too beautiful to be human, unearthly creatures arrested in flight, spellbound and absent even as their bodies remained deeply still.

"No offense," said Tim, "but the town you grew up in is Nowheresville."

We were back in the city. Tim, looking weary and harassed after an unexpected round of newsroom layoffs, paced the floor.

"Well, I'm not suggesting—" I said.

"Here, they're surrounded by bright, interesting people. They have concerts, museums, culture, cultural *diversity.* They have beaches, they can go sailing—"

"Sailing? These kids don't even have a backyard. Just to get some fresh air, they have to go three blocks and stay out of the way of fifteen other kids. You probably think that's 'gritty' or something, but Charles is two years old! I can't tell you the number of times some bigger boy has almost pushed him down."

"And what am I supposed to do? I'm a newsman, Cara. This is where the news *is.* You want me to go work at some two-bit local paper?"

"Not necessarily."

"Or take some stupid PR job because you can't handle life here and want to go hide under some rock? I've worked too hard—"

"Tim, look around. We can't provide a good life for these kids here. Your job pays practically nothing for all the work you do. You talk about the freaking *museums?* Every girl I went to high school with has her own washing machine, but I have to haul two kids and a laundry basket down two flights of stairs and have twelve quarters—"

"Well, no one's stopping you from going out and bringing in some money. When exactly are you planning to do that? Or are you just going to sit home and complain?"

"Oh! And who's supposed to take care of Charles and Bea? Do you want to hand them over to strangers five days a week? Most of my salary would go to paying other women to raise them. Is that your idea of the good life?"

"I'm not saying that. Three days, maybe. But you talk about how hard it is at home—"

"It is hard! You try it."

"Make up your mind. What do you want?"

"I want to get out of here," I said. "I want to get out of the city."

"And go where? With what jobs?"

We looked at each other for a long, icy moment. The baby started crying.

TICK TOCK, TICK TOCK.

The days were numbered, would never come back again. Charles was quickly outgrowing his clothes. Beatrice would not even remember being a baby. We moved through the vanishing hours like people in a dream.

We never intended to hurt them. We wanted to give them perfect lives, the best of everything.

If someone had asked us, at any point, what we would do for those children, Tim and I would have answered, "Anything!" without a moment's hesitation. We really thought we would do anything.

But we would have been lying.

14

THE THREE ORANGE BUTTERFLIES ARE BACK. THEY HOVER IN A GROUP, constantly changing position midair. It's like a choreographed dance. Kneeling on my bed, the best way I've found to be eye-level with the butterflies, I watched them for a long time out the window.

Group therapy still feels like a test I'm failing. The young therapist wants me to confess my feelings, tell my secrets. I've seen enough talk shows to know how to do this. But the context is all wrong, and my secrets, such as they are, don't really translate into therapeutic language. A foreign language I'm not sure I want to learn.

Some of the patients here have suffered awful traumas, and I feel humbled that they're willing to discuss their lives with strangers. The things they struggle with out in the world—addictions, abusive relationships, lost jobs, criminal pasts, a general inability to function—are abstractions to me, fates I have mysteriously been spared. Instead, I hit my marks, collected all the cards: college, white-collar job, handsome husband, healthy children. Still, while holding a royal flush, I fell apart. How to explain it?

Today, the therapist was wearing a button-down shirt, blazer, and slacks. While others talked, I spent a good while considering her outfit: all angles and clean lines, a corporate image of sexless efficiency. Even as a girl-reporter, I was too busty or too hippy for such clothes, the least flattering in my closet; my unruly lineaments were never straight. But she pulled off the look quite well. With her smooth hair and matching flats, she was neat as a pin.

"Cara, do you have anything to share today?"

I straightened in my chair, willing myself to make an effort. "I used to write about the movies," I began. "And I still think about movies quite a bit."

Around the circle, a dozen faces regarded me with mild interest.

"Go on," the therapist encouraged.

"Sometimes I wonder, how do we know…" I looked around, scanning the room for encouraging signs of sanity, "…that Cinderella lived happily ever after?"

The therapist smiled, as if she had been pitched an easy ball. "Well, it's a fairy tale, right? It's not meant to be taken seriously. In real life, as we know, *no* one lives—"

"But see, it's right there in the film," I interjected. "I'd always thought that, too. It's a dumb story, one that scams little girls into passively waiting for their prince. But then I re-watched it with my kids. It was the first time I'd seen it as an adult. And it's actually a lovely story with internal logic. Cinderella *is* going to live happily ever after. The entire plot functions to engineer her happiness."

"But we don't know what happens after her wedding," the therapist countered. "She and the prince ride off into the sunset, and that's it."

"It's been foreshadowed," I replied, getting into the conversation. Somebody had a coughing fit, probably detoxing, but I paid no attention. "What's Cinderella really like before the ball? She has a high tolerance for drudgery. She has a good attitude and enjoys the little things, like soap bubbles, most people wouldn't notice. And, in Disney's 1950 version, the iconic one we all know, she's always sewing clothes for mice and keeping them out of harm's way. The household mice love Cinderella! Because, on top of all her duties, she looks out for them and takes care of them. Which makes her perfect for the prince!"

The therapist now looked uncertain. Maybe she had been thrown a curveball after all. "Sorry, I don't follow. What do the mice have to do with the prince?"

"Why is he even getting married?" I exclaimed. "Because the king wants him to settle down and give him a grandchild. He's bored and wants to bounce a baby on his knee—the only real novelty there is, the one thing he can't buy. If the prince keeps gallivanting around, having adventures to no purpose, the king will never get his grandbaby. So, the king invites all the local girls to a fancy ball at the palace. It's all a scheme to get the prince married—not so the prince can get laid, or whatever, but so the kingdom can have a princess and an heir.

"Of course, it's nice if she's pretty. But they're recruiting a mother," I rattled on. "And who'll be a better mother than Cinderella? She's kind and loving and knows how to keep her cool while serving ingrates!"

I sat back in my chair. Maybe group therapy wasn't so bad after all.

"Then there's the bib," an unkempt old man piped up, raising a finger. "The bib… The older lady. *You* know."

"I'm sorry, Fred. I don't quite understand—" the therapist began.

"The bibbety-bobbety-boo lady," I offered. "Yes, exactly. Thank you, Fred."

"You're most welcome," Fred croaked and lowered his finger, satisfied.

"Cinderella's a born mother," I continued, warming to my theme, as if I were back in Tim's car dissecting *Fargo* with a beer on my lap. "But she has no mother herself. All she has is a wicked stepmother who hates her for her beauty. Just like the prince needs a father to nudge him into position, Cinderella requires a mother's help and guidance, or she'll be stuck being a servant to people who don't care about her. So, who comes along just at the right time? A magical godmother. She's cheery and plump, a bit flaky, not intimidating in the least. A *gentle* mother. Even though Cinderella messes up and doesn't leave the ball on time, it all turns out okay. The godmother's magic is enough. The couple's parents pull them both over the line. When we last see her, Cinderella is heading into a world that's literally waiting for her, a world that wants her just as she is. And that is why," I concluded, "we can believe she lives happily ever after."

The therapist put two fingertips to her temple, as if noticing the first twinges of a headache. "Thank you, Cara. You have an interesting take on things."

"That's what my husband said. Years ago, before he knew me very well. Of course," I added, as an unpleasant thought occurred to me, "the movie fails to account for the fact that evil is everywhere, waiting like a snare, even for Cinderella."

"Right. Okay, let's move on. Does anyone else have something to share?"

Dimly, I realized that I'd failed again.

I've got to start telling them what they want to hear, or they're never going to let me out.

15

"HAVE YOU MET MY SON?" ASKED TABITHA.

Something had happened to the air, an odd pocket of chill. We were standing by the lobby mailboxes, at the base of the winding staircase I didn't like. The children were upstairs with Tim.

Beside Tabitha stood a man of about forty, slightly built, with pale, thinning hair. Facially, he resembled his mother, but his expression was inward-looking while hers was curious and open. His mouth tugged upward in a smile, but he did not quite meet my eyes.

"I… No."

"Jeremy, Cara. Cara, Jeremy. Now you have. Cara has the most wonderful children! A little boy who just turned two and a new baby girl."

"Congratulations."

"Thanks."

"Jeremy's here helping me with my pesky foot."

"Your foot? What's wrong with it?"

"Oh, I don't want to bore you," Tabitha said staunchly. "Just the usual old-age nonsense. It's very tender and it hurts to walk, if you must know. So now I'm hobbling around like a decrepit old hag, aren't I, Jeremy?"

"I wouldn't say that, Mother. You just need a little help."

"Oh no. I'm sorry to hear that," I said. "Can I get you anything at the store? I'm just heading out now."

"No, no, no. I have everything I need." Tabitha waved a hand dismissively. "It's just a bother, that's all. I'm going in for surgery tomorrow."

"Surgery? Oh!"

"It's an outpatient procedure. No big deal. And don't worry, Mew has plenty of toys to keep her busy. Jeremy will keep an eye on her while I'm gone."

"I'm sure she'll be fine," I said. "Let me know if there's anything I can do."

"Jeremy works in the Geology Department at the university."

"That's sounds interesting. Are you a geologist?" I asked, turning toward him.

"Assistant to the Chair," he answered flatly.

"He handles all the paperwork of the department," Tabitha enthused. "Knows all the professors, an eccentric bunch."

"No doubt," I said, remembering my parents' faculty peers. It sounded like Jeremy functioned as their secretary. There was a pause as some weighted element of the conversation fell and settled.

"Well, I'm off to the store—" I began.

"Don't let us keep you," Tabitha said at the same time.

"Tabitha." I turned back toward her on an impulse. "I'm sorry you have to go through this. With your foot. If there's anything—"

"Thank you, Cara. You take care of those babies!" And with that, she stepped gingerly into the elevator with a smile.

A STRANGE THING HAS HAPPENED TO ME. I HESITATE TO WRITE IT DOWN.

I sat on a wooden park bench by the lake, graffiti carved into its peeling surface. Two plastic drugstore bags containing baby wipes, Q-tips, toothpaste, and an aspirational tube of lipstick rested beside me, contents baking in the sun.

Even in the cramped and smelly circus of our lives, where personal mystery was at a fantastically low ebb, I'd discovered it was possible to have secrets. The trick was to get out of the house, to slip its surly bonds. And that was why I would occasionally make a show of packing up my yoga mat or some overdue library books and, with an air of fond reluctance, bid my family *au revoir* and go and smoke.

At the drugstore, I'd bought the most expensive pack of cigarettes they had. Its pretty box and silver foil were like a birthday present—a present from someone who was trying to kill me by slow degrees, but festive nonetheless. I had a complex relationship with its pretentious label. Marketers somewhere were trying to get me to associate their product with glamour and sophistication, and I saw right through that but nonetheless *did* associate their product with glamour and sophistication. Because smoking expensive cigarettes was awesome. No one could place a hand on me with their bodily needs or bourgeois morality. I was off the grid, incommunicado, destroying my own cells with relish.

Today, I was also writing in a small notebook. It felt like a throwback to my old life, a life of words, words, words. The husk of my logical mind, hollowed out by hundreds of hours of lost sleep, was trying fitfully to reason. Focus.

I think maybe it has something to do with my brain?

Exhaling a column of smoke, I pondered my own brain. Something had changed, something no one told me about. Searching for clues, I had been reading up on the subject. *During pregnancy, the brain shrinks about six percent... possibly becoming more efficient... . Blood is shunted away from the forebrain toward the hindbrain, which controls survival... Short-term memory is affected... A hormonal cascade that shifts her into fight-or-flight mode... Ability to respond to infants' needs and to detect threatening people in their environment... Might confer an adaptive advantage... Changes last for at least two years... Dramatic neuroplasticity... Alterations may become more pronounced with each successive pregnancy... Scientists do not fully understand at this time...*

The most I wrote by hand was a grocery list, and I could barely read my own writing anymore.

Since I came home from the hospital with Bea (but starting with Charles)

And even more when I returned to the city after a week away

It always hit me when I walked into the building. Out on the streets, it was a low, uncomfortable hum of awareness, a stress headache of the emotions. I couldn't get a precise read. But in the apartment building, where a few dozen people lived out their lives—ate, slept, sat transfixed by their screens, struggled, dreamed, despaired, year after year—a troubled feeling-tone permeated the jewel-toned carpet, the staircase connecting the lobby and mezzanine, the dripping sink in the sun-washed laundry room, the dim interior corridors, the fire escapes on every floor.

There is something wrong with everybody here.
The stairs wanted me to drop Charles, or I thought they did?
It is in 3C.
I can feel it seeping into the apartment, through the walls.

SUNLIGHT, BIRDSONG, A SUMMER DAY. PEOPLE WERE STROLLING PAST the lake, playing frisbee, lying on blankets. I checked the time. I really should be getting home.

The woman we called the Angry Ballerina was bone-thin with dyed black hair, her posture brittle and erect. She lived just down the hall, and as Tim and I grappled two fussing kids and all their gear into the elevator, she would reliably emerge in a black unitard and purse her lips at us, her least favorite neighbors.

Marguerite is full of bitterness and rage. Decades ago, her husband left her for her student, and she broods on this every day, creating elaborate fantasies of revenge.

The pair downstairs we called the Mother and Middle-Aged Daughter were quiet and polite. The elder did bookkeeping, and the younger, a heavyset woman in her mid-thirties, taught middle school.

Francine is stealing money from her employer off the books. It pays for her designer clothes, her trips to the salon. She feels like she deserves it because life has treated her badly.

Emma secretly hates her mother. She never wanted a be a teacher, but Francine pressured her into it: a sensible job for a woman. She longs to be free, outdoors, away from children. Only food loves her back.

Not long ago, I'd run into the Aesthete swinging open the lobby door early on a Saturday morning. Carrying two paper coffee cups in a tray, he seemed surprised to see me. Taking one look at him, I'd stepped back as if I'd touched a hot wire.

"Brighton?"

"Oh, hello! Sorry, can't talk. I have to take an important call!"

Brighton brings people home to show off his music, art collection, books. Most of his guests are needy, lonely. And some of them are far too young.

Not everyone's aura was strong. Some gave off the merest impression of a gap or space inside, a flute of nothingness, a deep and unseen cavity. Their personalities swirled, oblivious, around the hole, which waited to be filled with something that was not-them. The vacant hole was patient…

Everywhere I look, evil is.

Beneath the bone, under the surface

My pencil paused above the page. I thought about Tabitha's son, Jeremy Brown. It wasn't evil I sensed in him, exactly. It was weakness.

"Someone named Erin needs to talk to you!" I called. It was the next day, a Sunday.

After a moment, Tim emerged from the bathroom, where he'd been shaving. The electric razor purring in his hand, he turned it off and said politely, "What?"

"I was looking for the checkbook on your desk. There's a work e-mail on your screen. It just came in. Subject line: I need to talk to you. Sounds important! Have you paid the electric bill, by any chance?"

"Just a colleague," said Tim. "Probably about a story."

"Did you pay it, though? Make my day."

"What? No."

"Do we have money left to pay it?"

"I don't know."

Five minutes later, Tim slammed his laptop shut. "Stupid work e-mails," he groused in my direction. "You'd think they'd let me have one day at home, sans drama." He zipped the computer into a case and put it away. "Now, who wants a smoothie? I'm in the mood to blend all of a sudden. Cara? How about it?"

I REALIZE THAT WRITING THIS FROM A PSYCHIATRIC HOSPITAL MAKES me a poor source on the subject of the ants, but I swear it happened. At least, I was sure at the time I wasn't dreaming.

Admittedly, it began in deep, dreamless sleep, on the cracked leather couch. With Charles gone, the apartment was weirdly still. Tim had taken him to run errands, and Bea was down for a nap, miraculously dozing in her crib for once. My body felt light without her in the pouch, and I curled up on the stiff cushions, every cell reveling in the luxury of shutting down. To the sound of soothing music, wordless and foreign in its rhythms, I descended swiftly into blackness.

Sometime later, I was conscious of a new song on the stereo, a gentle male voice singing over what sounded like a Brazilian street band. The song was about an infant girl found in a basket among the reeds of a riverbank, both like and unlike some ancient story I couldn't place.

Was the baby awake? I thought I heard a whimper under the music.

I lifted a sleep-heavy hand and rubbed my eyes. The baby was crying softly. How long had she been awake?

"Bunchy?"

Beneath the singer's soft voice, an electric guitar pulsed a forward-moving beat. The lyrics circled back, picked up by a choir of voices that seemed to jump between the speakers on the far wall. A song of innocence and experience, about an infant gazing up at an adult. I saw that Tim had rigged some kind of curtain across the bedroom door before he left, though we had never talked about a curtain. Oddly, it appeared to be moving.

"Beatrice?" I said, rising.

Two days ago, a trail of sugar ants had appeared along the floorboards. It was unclear where they had entered, since we were four floors up, but a thin, single-file line tracked through the living room, around the dining room, and into the kitchen. I didn't have the bandwidth to care about the ants and so, except for stashing away a few things on the counter, I did nothing, choosing to view them as a fascinating natural phenomenon. Hopefully, they would be gone in a few days, disappearing as mysteriously as they'd arrived.

The curtain was made of mesh or small, dark beads. What was Tim thinking? It hung in the doorway, floor to ceiling, seeming to ripple in the light.

Bea was really crying now.

"I'm coming!"

Approaching the bedroom, I suddenly stepped back with a shriek. Millions of black ants filled the doorway like a beaded curtain, a dense matrix of pencil-thin lines suspended in mid-air. A thick, orderly swarm in constant motion.

How long did I pause there? Five seconds? My hands clenched in deep, physical shock. My mouth fell open. And then I realized I had to get the baby.

I spun around to the front closet, tore a raincoat off its hanger and threw it over my head like a cloak. "Hang on," I called. "I'll be right there." Eyes closed tight, I ran through the ants and, with a scream, let the raincoat fall to the ground.

Bea was in her crib, sound asleep.

Stunned, I looked back up at the doorway. Nothing. Empty.

16

I'M TRYING TO TELL THE TRUTH, BUT I HAVEN'T BEEN ENTIRELY HONEST.
I've said that Tim and I were always tired during those first years with Charles, and when he finally started sleeping through the night, Bea came along. Every night, while Tim read storybooks to Charles in the bedroom, I paced the living room, jogging the baby on one shoulder, singing all the children's songs I could recall. Some of the nursery rhymes I'd learned as a toddler, from a Mother Goose book illustrated with pigs and cats, seemed vaguely sinister as I warbled them into Bea's ear, as if I'd misremembered them in a delirious trick of the mind.

London Bridge is falling down, falling down, falling down,
London Bridge is falling down, my fair lady.
Take the key and lock 'er up, lock 'er up, lock 'er up…

So yes, I sleepwalked through whole hours, even days, cutting grapes lengthwise at the counter with a thousand-mile stare. But some of it was my own fault. Some nights, I forced myself to stay awake until I was the last one standing. I waited for Tim, Charles, and Bea to finally sack out, so that only one conscious mind blipped and pulsed in the darkened apartment, because it was the only way I could escape. And I desperately needed to escape.

So, wearing earmuff-like headphones and my pajamas, I watched classic films on a laptop while my husband and kids slept. Deep in a nest of blankets on the leather couch, a bowl of popcorn by my side, it felt like an illicit midnight date—albeit in my own home, with myself. For both my physical and mental health, I should have been asleep. But some stubborn part of me refused to stop imagining, pretending, even now.

I watched *That Hamilton Woman* and *A Streetcar Named Desire* and *Waterloo Bridge*, in which an exquisite, fragile Vivien Leigh burned with nervous energy. Drifting into an Elizabeth Taylor phase, I watched *A Place in the Sun* and *Butterfield 8* and *Suddenly, Last Summer* and

Giant, the last of which evoked a hankering for Westerns—all that open land, all that sky. This led to *High Noon* and *The Man Who Shot Liberty Valance*. After a long, wearying day, I pivoted to lighter fare: *Breakfast at Tiffany's* and *The Princess Bride* and *Moonstruck*. I was almost ready to the turn the corner into mystery and suspense...

When I moved Bea aside at two or three a.m. and squeezed into the family bed, my imagination felt refreshed, a scraggly, half-dead plant after a rainstorm. Some alchemy had taken place so that, for a few hours, I'd lived another life, seeing through the eyes of a character—usually, a woman—whose hope, fear, longing, and ambivalence I experienced moment by moment. It was the oddest thing; I never could explain it. Remote in time and space, she seemed to be as close as my own breath. Though we had never met, she was, somehow, magically, both me and herself.

MEANWHILE, BAD THINGS WERE HAPPENING IN THE CITY. EVERY DAY, three local newspapers arrived at our apartment, allowing Tim to keep tabs on the competition. So it was impossible to avoid the headlines, bleeding and leading every week. Two women's burned corpses were discovered in a weedy, abandoned lot. One Saturday afternoon, a nine-year-old boy was taking a piano lesson when a stray bullet burst through the music store's wall, instantly paralyzing him from the chest down. A burly dog got loose and mauled an elderly neighbor to death. A banker hung himself at the edge of the lake at dawn, presumably facing the water, taking the scenic route. I knew the spot well and sometimes stopped there with Charles.

Into the dangerous world I leapt

What was the verse? Only a fragment floated up from buried memory. Cross-legged on the rug, I picked up spongy blocks and dropped them into a repurposed laundry hamper filled with toys.

Something something my father wept
Into the dangerous world I leapt

Tim was reclining in a nearby chair, his legs spread wide. He was saying something about college. "And we have to consider out-of-state, or private..."

"Can you move your foot?" I interjected. He rested his right foot on his left knee, allowing me to grab a block from under his chair. "Thanks."

"But obviously, without a second income, we can't afford to start his college fund right now. And, with another kid already—which is great, don't get me wrong—we're going to need two savings accounts."

"*Like a fiend hid in a cloud*," I recited, suddenly remembering.

From his high perch, Tim shot me a disgusted look. I didn't care. I had no interest in being the girl Tim liked: an early, more pliable version of myself, new to the city and eager to please. It seemed unfair that this was still the thing he wanted. I was twenty pounds heavier, leaking milk; my pencil-skirt days were long gone. The city exhausted and frightened me, but he wouldn't leave. Instead, he was trying to *guilt* me into going back to work, playing on my supposed love of education.

But did I love it? Several years post-graduation, I wasn't sure. Some of the things I'd learned were ricocheting back, freshly disturbing.

Into the dangerous world I leapt
Helpless, naked, piping loud
Like a fiend hid in a cloud.

"Never mind. I can see you're busy," Tim said acidly, standing up.

"I am, actually. You're welcome to come down and help."

After Tim stalked away, I turned to Bea, who was propped nearby in a small vibrating chair. "That's William Blake," I told her.

She tugged one of her pant legs up, showing a sturdy leg ending in a white sock.

"I don't know about you, Bunch," I said, tossing a block into the bin. "I don't know if you're ever going to be employable. What company would want to hire you? You're what they call"—I made air quotes with my fingers—"an 'oddball.'"

Beatrice blinked and smiled.

AS CALAMITIES SWEPT THE CITY, I ROCKED IN MY CHAIR, KEEPING AN eye on Charles. Most of his two-year-old peers spent weekdays in day care, or—as working parents called the better, more expensive day cares—"school." If I went back to full-time work, Charles would swap his formless hours around the house for a rousing day of finger-painting, singing, outdoor play, circle time, alphabet-chanting, sharing, and learning about the seasons while munching organic snacks.

I had nothing against all this. Still, I preferred to have both kids with me. I simply liked seeing their faces: a hard-earned privilege I didn't want to give away. I liked to talk to them, to make Bea laugh, to watch Charles frown with concentration with his toy phone pressed to one ear or impatiently turn the pages of a book he knew by heart. So, instead of constructing kites out of recycled paper or counting to ten in Spanish, Charles spent his days close to his mom, running experiments on the rules governing his world. If he dribbled into the kiddie potty seat, he got an M&M. If he painted himself with mayonnaise, he got rebuked, wiped down, and plopped unceremoniously in his crib. He was rarely out of my sight, and I was rarely out of his.

I tried to be a calm presence, and sometimes I was genuinely happy. But I couldn't shake a preoccupying sensation of unease, even dread. There was a hole at the center of things, an empty chamber where the night winds howled. Every person entered the world *like a fiend hid in a cloud*. Whatever thrummed beneath the city's streets would come for us eventually, taking a form I couldn't foresee and couldn't control.

Even at this moment, it rushed toward Charles on swift, silent wings. I mulled this while watching him smear his highchair tray with marinara sauce or move a plastic boat across the surface of his bath. I was just one frail, ordinary person, and my years guarding Charles would be brief. One day, I would watch him leap, alone, into the dangerous world. If only I could pass the baton to someone who could get to him anywhere, at any time: trapped in the rubble of an exploded subway train in darkness, or alone in a crowded bar and weathering some private agony.

Was God, at bottom, a conspiracy of mothers? Maybe we'd all had the same realization, over the millennia, about the impossibility of protecting our sons: rebels and daredevils from the get-go, born to trouble as the sparks fly upward. We could perhaps keep the girls close, but wherever our boys were going, we couldn't follow. Maybe we collectively dreamed up God over our looms and cooking fires, demanded he exist, and tasked him with looking after our children in all the places where we couldn't reach them. What mother wouldn't want an omnipresent super-parent to exist?

My job, over the coming years, was to impart things to the children that would bring them aid and comfort. Ideally—and this was the tricky part—these things would also be true. Maybe I should drag all four of us into church, a real church that actually believed things, for whose members heaven and hell gaped all around in invisible, thrilling realms of awe and terror. Was *this* the answer?

We had, in fact, been to church some months ago, a sort of field trip. It was a new cathedral, modern and ambitious, raised on the shore of the lake while Charles and I, in our perambulations, looked on from below. One night in December, shortly after it opened, we stopped by to see what it was like on the inside.

The four of us were driving home from some errand, and no one was eager to get back to our cluttered, cramped apartment. On a whim, we pulled up to the church. Tim left us in the car with the heater running while he went inside to make sure it was open, then emerged to give a thumbs-up. With an air of adventure, we hauled the kids out of their car seats and swung Charles up the steps, the baby affixed to my chest: a merry little band of pilgrims. Like the few other times Tim and I had visited a church for someone's wedding or piano concert, it felt transgressive, by far the edgiest thing we'd done all week.

Inside loomed a cavernous space with a few dozen people in the pews. A priest was wrapping up some business at the front, speaking—as best we could tell—Korean. We stood in the back, gawking like the tourists we were. The chapel was stark and austere, not to my taste. Its walls were rough and gray like cinderblock, vaguely suggestive of the world as prison camp—a notion that seemed theologically unsound. The sacred art was simple and abstract, almost primitive. I would have preferred kitsch and baubles, banks of cheap flowers, gold and filigree, like being inside a giant wedding cake; a service punctuated with inside jokes and ending with the flinging of confetti. Instead, even the Christmas tree in the front hall was minimalist, tasteful.

After a few minutes, we left. But as we coaxed Charles down the back steps, something caught my eye. Silvery and slender, catching the moonlight like a strand of spider's web, it was a construction ladder bolted onto the side of the church and stretching up past the roof, piercing the night sky. Just looking at it made me queasy. It was too narrow, reached too high. I couldn't imagine who could climb it. They'd have to cling to the rungs, keeping their gaze up or straight ahead, the city blazing all around in a dizzying whirl of lights.

Tim and I had an unspoken agreement that, some evenings, no matter how disastrous the apartment, no matter how fussy the kids were being, I could, occasionally, disappear for an hour or two. I say "unspoken" but should add that I mentioned it often and at length, in varying keys of bitterness or desperation, and with the fluency and passion of a Cicero, a Churchill, until Tim was like, "Whatever. Just go!"

This was such a night.

As usual, I had no agenda. I was but a leaf on the wind. I could visit a coffee shop, a bookstore, a restaurant, a shoe boutique, a wine bar, a flower market, a nail salon, or countless other spots, but instead headed toward my favorite place in the city: the cemetery.

Verdant and huge, speckled with headstones like pebbles on a beach, it occupied a forty-acre swath of land in a nice part of town, a pricey neighborhood of shops and restaurants. I was surprised the dead could hold their own against Subway and Starbucks. Yet, here they were: soldiers, bankers, brides, cooks, infants, and grandmothers, arrayed in unbreachable, stalwart rows, dead set against all offers.

Unlike the city, the graveyard seemed inspired by lofty principles. Comprised mostly of empty space, its green acres felt airy and expansive, an escape from some invisible cage. A harmonious landscape of grass, trees, and stones had been arranged around some rogue common desire that had nothing to do with getting and spending. Silent and still, the cemetery felt like a secret city nestled within the larger one, a counter-city with a cryptic counter-message. Here and there, tall stone figures stood watch: winged women, somber children, statues embodying both gentleness and vigilance.

Few people were around that night. The sun was setting. I motored down a random path and pulled the car over to one side. Three minutes later, I was sitting on a curb next to the immaculate resting place of ANNA LOUISE HODGE (1906-1954). Lighting a cigarette, I felt the unhassled mild despair that, these days, passed for peace.

For a long while, I turned things over in mind: how my marriage was becoming terse and distant, how I'd spanked Charles in anger when he broke into the refrigerator and upended a giant tub of yogurt, how I could not bring myself to apply for jobs even though we were running out of money, how being cooped up all day in the apartment with my own children could make me feel as cruelly trapped as Anne Frank, how getting through each day seemed harder than I had ever expected, how there was no respite or help if I was not up to the task. Later, I walked among the graves, the taste of ashes in my mouth.

Before too long, I had to leave, as we were out of Bea-sized diapers and I needed to stop by Walgreens before going home to relieve Tim of solo duty during dinner, bath, and bedtime.

On the way out, I passed plots marked JONES, OSTERHOLM, LEVY, ZHANG, and VARGAS. Entire families were buried side by side under one tall ancestral stone. Unlike us, they were not so quick to be rid of each other. They did not opt to end their time on earth as a boxful of ashes poured into the ocean, like my grandmother; heaved into some field, like Tim's grandfather; strewn atop some mountain, like my aunt; raked under some tree, like my cousin; pitched into some reef, like my great-uncle; or cannonballed into the swirling depths of space, like my grandfather. Instead, they piled their coffins under one rock and stayed put, forever.

I was impressed with them, these families. The sheer persistence of their resting bones.

17

"I spy, with my little eye..."

Flee squinted into the distance, across a manicured lawn bordered by a high wall. If you listened, you could hear the Doppler waves of freeway traffic—a thousand cars and trucks approaching and receding—on the other side. A few patients wandered the grounds, smudges of dull color on the green grass. Flee and I shared a cast-iron bench, old-fashioned in style, as if we were feeding pigeons in a London park. Flee cast her gaze around and then tilted her face up toward the sky.

"...something white."

"A cloud," I guessed.

"Yep. Your turn."

"I spy, with my little eye..."

Flee was looking better today, more put-together. She had done something different with her hair. Though she still hummed, she hadn't sung about the Devil in three days.

"...something purple."

"Those flowers, what are they called?" said Flee. "The one from the Van Gogh. Irises."

"Right."

She turned to me and considered me quizzically for a moment. "You don't tell them everything, do you?"

"What do you mean?"

"Everything you spy with your little eye. Be careful what you say. They will pretend to understand, but they will be very confused. It just drags everything out, trust me."

I nodded, pretending to understand. "Seems like you're feeling better," I ventured.

"Yeah. I was so tired when I got here. So exhausted. I couldn't sleep and being awake felt like being crushed. I hated being awake. I just couldn't do it anymore."

This time, I didn't have to pretend to understand.

"But I feel like I'm improving," she continued. "They've taken good care of me here, as best they can. I spy, with my little eye… something black. Oh!"

I turned to look in the direction she was gazing. Two figures were walking across the lawn in our direction: a female orderly in blue and a man in a black shirt and pants. They were chatting as they approached, the woman talking, the man nodding. They stopped in front of Flee and me.

"Kit Fletcher?" the woman said. "You have a visitor."

I looked at Flee. She looked surprised, half-smiling.

"There she is!" the man said in heavily accented English. He was slightly built, brown-skinned, and balding. I placed his age somewhere between 28 and 45.

"Wow. You came to see me," said Flee.

"Of course, of course. We were all very worried about you. I'm Father Ray," the man said, turning to me. "I've known Kit since she was a small girl."

"I'm going to head back," the orderly said. "The room is ready if you need it." She gave a nod to Flee and then lumbered away over the lawn.

"It's all right that I came, I hope?"

"Yeah. Of course. This is my friend, Cara."

"Good to meet you." He bent his head at me like someone who hailed from a more formal culture. "Are you an artist, too, by any chance?"

"Oh, no," I said. "I'm not anything, really. Just a mom."

The priest squinted at me, tracing a half-circle in the air around my face. "You have a bit of that look…" he murmured. "I thought you might know each other from the Academy."

"No. Just from here," I replied, feeling foolish. This conversation seemed to be over my head.

"Kit's very talented." He smiled, revealing slightly crooked teeth. "Admitted to the Academy at fifteen. The youngest ever, I believe."

"But I keep getting sick," said Flee, rubbing her forehead with one hand. "I do all right there for a while, but…"

"I hope you are taking your medicine," the priest said to Flee an avuncular tone. "You have to take it, yes?"

"I guess," said Flee glumly.

"No 'I guess!'" barked the priest. "How can you do your work like this?"

"What kind of art do you do?" I asked to break the tension, but also out of real curiosity.

"Photorealism." Flee sounded bored with the word, as if she had said it too many times.

"You would not believe her pictures were painted," Father Ray said to me. "She has great skill. They appear very real. Like a reflection in a mirror. Except, if you look closely…" He glanced at Flee, as if uncertain whether to reveal a secret.

"Go on," she said.

"…they're full of schools. Once you see all the schools, you can't *not* see them."

I turned questioningly to Flee.

"Skulls," she corrected.

"Schools! That's what I said." Father Ray smiled and clasped his hands together. "Kit, I am here to hear your confession, if you'd like."

There was a pause in which the odds of this happening seemed low. I knew Flee to be distrustful and cagey. Hadn't she just advised me not to tell everything?

"Okay," she said.

"Okay, good. They've set a private room aside." Flee hopped off the bench, and they both turned toward the building. As an afterthought, Father Ray turned back to me. "Would you also like to make your confession?"

"Oh, no," I said. "I'm fine, thank you."

Flee waved good-bye, revealing a wrist crisscrossed by scars usually hidden within a sleeve. Her expression was hard to read. Relief, maybe, or simple acquiescence. Once more, I realized how young she was, hardly more than a child.

"Very nice meeting you," said Father Ray.

I watched them walk away over the grass, two thin figures in black.

18

"I was born in America," I said around the Fourth of July, months before my hospitalization. "My children were born in America. You, if your mother is to be believed on this point, were born in America. So why are we living like people who were smuggled into this country in the back of a van?"

"That's enough," said Tim, who didn't go in for ethnic humor. I only said such things around Tim, jokes that stemmed no more from real ill feeling than any other type of joke. (After all, my own father had been an immigrant.) At least poverty-stricken newcomers had an excuse to cram entire families into one small, packed bedroom humid with bodily emissions. We were two college-educated citizens who had enjoyed every advantage. What was the matter with us? If we were so smart, why weren't we rich?

We were looking sporadically for a new place to live, but every time we toured a home in our price range, it left me deeply shaken. Emblematic of this experience was the wild-eyed owner of a crumbling Victorian with Tibetan peace flags on a drooping string across the porch, her ponytail half-dyed pink and half gunmetal gray, a snub-faced dog the color of muddy water nosing at her heels, who said to Tim after a walk-through, lingering convivially on the stoop:

"Bad Rep. Have you heard of it?"

"Pardon?" said Tim.

"Bad Rep? Are you familiar with that organization—as a journalist, I mean?"

"No, I'm not."

"The couple two doors down, a younger couple. They run it out of their house. It's a great organization! They take in pit bulls from neglectful homes. That's where I got Rusty here."

"Come on, Charles," I said sharply, tightening my grip on the baby. "Tim. It was nice meeting you! Tim?"

"We'll call and let you know," said Tim. "Did I see solar panels on the roof? That's fascinating—"

"*Tim.*"

"It has potential," he said as we approached the car. "Though you'd have to go back to work for us to even think about it."

"Are you kidding me?"

"What? It's a fixer-upper."

"Let's just get the kids buckled in and get out of this neighborhood. There was a pair of women's underwear on the sidewalk, all balled up. It looked like it had been there a while."

"That was men's underwear."

"You're thinking about the other one, next to the mailbox, or what I guess used to be the mailbox. The mailbox *post.*"

"I see your point."

"You know," I said. We were several minutes into the loading session, him working furiously to tie down Charles while I tied down the other one. "One day, we won't have to strap the kids into anything. They'll just hop in the backseat, put on their seat belts, and off we'll go. I know it's hard to believe now—"

"I don't believe it," Tim said grimly.

"When we meet on that beautiful shore," I went on dreamily. "When we don't have to cinch anyone into a five-point harness."

"Will I even recognize you then?" asked Tim, giving a final, decisive tug to a neon-colored strip of nylon.

"I don't think we'll have bodies anymore," I mused over the baby's wails and a sharp click. "Only spirits. Or is that the gnostic heresy? I can't remember from undergrad."

"Hand me my pomegranate juice," said Tim.

We climbed inside and shut the doors, a capsule of Nielsens preparing to rocket onto the freeway and then to the store—the fancy one, where every manner of delicacy awaited us. Occasionally, I compared my life to that of my grandmother, who spent two decades in a red brick house across from her kids' school. This memory added to the impression I often had in the city that we were outrageously privileged and, at the same time, serfs without a groat to our names or a pot to piss in. Tim and Cara Nielsen and their children: peasants, nobodies.

EVERY GENERATION MUST FEEL ITSELF THE VICTIM OF A FATAL LACK OF information, must feel increasingly aggrieved that the truths it received were incomplete. Crucial points were left out, key elements glossed over or diminished, the rest riddled with inconsistencies, with biases, with error. Were we to *live* by this ramshackle assortment of platitudes? No one could do it. It was impossible. Demonstrably, the world did not yield to such poor stuff.

What was it they forgot to tell us? No one could quite put their finger on it. We were like people who had learned the alphabet from Scrabble tiles: missing an *O*, lacking a *T*, clutching a useless *X*. The box rattled, the letters turned up as they would: randomly. Surely *home* was a word, but we had *hum* and unusable *hume*.

"One, two, fwee," Charles said often, apropos of nothing.

When we were kids, the grown-ups had seemed so breezy, so assured. Yet, now that *we'd* grown up, we all seemed to be floundering in ignorance. Life was not really all that fun, though certainly fun had been intimated. Things were not really all that hard—or all that easy, come to think of it. Paper or plastic? This or that? What did it matter? Were we idiots? Had we been groomed and trained for something that was not quite human life?

An entire hapless generation now boiled down to me and Tim, indoors and four floors up with our kids. Charles lounged around the apartment all day, sucking a pacifier and issuing demands to watch *Bob the Builder*, which played more or less on a continuous loop. Each show began with a theme song containing the lusty refrain, "Can we fix it? *Yes! We! Can!*"

Bob and his friends stated the point a shade too forcefully, I felt. Had anyone asked me the same question, whether about a clogged sink or democratic capitalism or the human enterprise as a whole, my answer would have been, "Maybe a little," or, "Probably not." Tim would have thought the whole thing hinged on expertise, intelligently deployed. Charles, for his part, appeared to like things broken—

preferably by him. Meanwhile, the baby was as yet blissfully ignorant that anything was wrong. So there we were, the four of us, none of us really on board with Bob. Yet Charles seemed drugged by his adventures in usefulness, so we kept it on.

"Dada," he said once, pointing at the screen.

"Does Bob remind you of Daddy?" I inquired.

"Yah."

"Well, your dad hasn't built a lot of stuff around this place," I remarked dryly. "Except a mountain of resentment in my heart."

A moment passed.

"Honey?" I asked.

Nothing.

"Honey? Did you catch that?"

"Yeah. That's funny," said Tim.

"I'LL HAVE THE MINCHET ABISH WOT."

"I'll do the Assa Gored," said Gemma virtuously, as it was fish.

"Okay. Did you want those after the Missir Shorba and Timatim Fitfit? Or just as they're ready?"

"As they're ready."

"And a honey wine, please," I added.

"Two honey wines," said Gemma.

"And two waters."

"Sparkling or tap?"

"Sparkling."

"Tap."

The waitress nodded, her hands folded. Having committed all to memory, no pen in sight, she receded gracefully behind a painted screen.

Gemma and I smiled at each other over a small, round table at the Ethiopian restaurant down the hill from my building. Gemma carried herself differently now; she had a new self-confidence or self-regard. It suited her somehow, made her seem glamorous and remote. She had just moved in with Vivek—they had kicked all the roommates out—and had the rosy glow of someone planning a major remodel.

"The kitchen is garbage," she confided after a swig of honey wine. "Old, gross appliances—not retro old, just old—pressed-wood cabinets, no prep sink, not even an island. Tiny window. Obviously designed by a man!"

This was my cue for some expression of female solidarity. All I could think of was *and paid for by a man*, but this seemed petty and unworthy of us both. Instead, I cocked my head, unsure how to arrange my face or what to say.

After the brief pause that ensued, Gemma asked brightly, "So, how about you guys? Find anything to buy yet?"

"It's been pretty grim, to be honest. Prices in the city are just... I don't know how anyone does it."

"You could always move to the suburbs." She rattled off a few locations, reasonably near as the crow flew but lashed to the city by roads lousy with traffic at all hours, roads whose sheer hellishness was legendary, world-famous. People died idling in their cars, and it didn't even make the news.

"We've looked into it," I said slowly. "The thing is, Tim's hours are...irregular. Right now he's ten minutes from home, but if we lived that far away, we'd hardly see him."

"Could he telecommute? Some of Vivek's employees live on the beach or are basically ski bums. They work insane hours remotely, but they're a mile from the slopes."

"Well, it's a newsroom. It's old-fashioned—literally a room. I'm not sure Tim would even want to work from home. I think he likes the energy of being at work."

"What about you, though?"

"I don't know. We really need a bigger place. I keep hoping Tim will get another job and be willing to move. Every time I see housing prices somewhere else, I feel like a chump."

"Is he looking for other jobs?"

"No."

"Why not?"

"He says he's too busy with work."

Gemma rolled her eyes, and for a second, I caught a glimpse of my marriage from her perspective. It didn't look good.

"How was your trip to India?" I asked, realizing in that instant that Gemma knew more about my dad's country than I did. I'd never been there, though every other summer my father had flown home alone. By that time, Claudia hardly traveled anymore. And now it seemed unlikely I would ever go.

"So amazing," said Gemma, brightening. "Vivek's cousin was this adorable girl, ninety pounds probably. Just exquisite, covered in jewels. And the wedding lasted three days! The groom rode in on a white horse. Feasts every night for all the guests—five hundred of them! I learned the *bhangra* and we killed it on the dance floor. Gorgeous explosions of flowers, crazy food. It was great!"

"Wow. Is Vivek's family rich?"

"I think they're ordinary." Gemma shrugged. "That's just how it goes over there."

"It sounds fantastic. It's just weird that it's so elaborate. All that money just to get married? They should save it to buy a house, to hire help when they have kids. You can get married at City Hall!"

"Well, it was interesting to see," said Gemma primly. "In case Vivek and I ever, you know. The worst part was the flight."

"Oh?"

"Going was fine, I just took an Ambien and slept. But on the way back, we sat in front of this frigging kid, this little *maniac*—"

"Uh oh."

"Kicking the seat for seven hours. His mom was like"—she switched to a weak, mincing voice—"*'Stop it, I'm sorry, I'm so sorry.'* But did he stop it, ever? No. And every third time, he'd start whining, literally screeching in my ear. Did this kid not ever hear 'no' before? What's wrong with the parents? Don't they know this is why people hate kids on planes?"

"Hmm. That sounds tough."

"It's like, hello? If your brat can't behave, leave him home already! Don't inflict him on the rest of us, lady. These tickets weren't cheap!"

"Maybe they were taking him to see family, and there was just no other—"

"Family can wait until they get that mess under control. Seriously, there should be a rule. It's not fair to the other passengers."

"No. I guess not."

Gemma put down her empty wine glass, breathed deeply and seemed to gather herself anew. "I'm sure your kids wouldn't be like that."

"Well, we don't fly much anyway," I said.

As we smiled across the table, it dawned on me that I was not going to call Gemma again. And she was not going to call me again. I didn't have time or energy to spend on someone stupid about kids. And from where she sat, I was too burdened and too broke to be fun anymore.

Gently, the waitress laid down the black wallet of the check on the white cloth.

"It's been great catching up," I said.

"It really has."

A HOUSE BEING IMPOSSIBLE, I LOBBIED FOR A CAR. MY PREVIOUS CAR, like my bicycle, had been stolen years ago: stripped of its copper wire as it sat on our street, and not worth fixing. Since then, we'd shared the one car: Tim's.

In the city, I'd learned, whatever crimes or indignities might have been inflicted on one's person in a less civilized place and time—a lawless Hobbesian world of all against all—were now inflicted on one's car. While in small towns and on the open roads, cars actually got you someplace, in the city they functioned largely as hostility-absorbing devices, shields against the inchoate rage and disregard of fellow citizens. There were too few police to care that your car had been scarred and robbed and joyridden and ditched by the side of the road. And because the city itself was only too eager to levy taxes, fines, and fees on your car for doing things a car could not help but do, like park, the city went ahead and kicked it around too. After all, the car was not going to write a letter to the editor or stage a protest outside City Hall or set itself on fire with the news cameras rolling, because it was just a freaking *car* and helpless as a baby sparrow. Owning a car was supposed to be fun! It was supposed to mean freedom, endless travel possibilities! But it was not fun in the city. Honestly, city people felt sorry for cars. However crammed with pointless difficulties their own lives were, cars had it worse.

"Why, again, do you want a car?" asked Tim. He felt that owning two cars was not green.

"Because I feel trapped!" I said. "If I had my own car, I could go places by myself without some schedule or negotiation, just spur of the moment. And you would still have your car for the kids."

"You wouldn't take the kids?"

"No. That would defeat the purpose. But you'd have a car, for emergencies."

"But you don't even like to drive! You make me drive you everywhere, even to Target. Are you saying you would drive your *own* car to Target?"

"No. I don't like driving on freeways, and Target is too far and even the surface roads are crowded. It makes me nervous just getting near that place, so you'll still have to take me. The point is—"

"But—"

"The point is that I have no sense of freedom, no autonomy. I'm stuck in these three rooms all day, and I need to be able to just walk out the door and drive somewhere."

"But you don't drive. That's what I'm saying."

"Of course I drive. I drive around the neighborhoods. I drive to—" I named the upscale area with a hillside cemetery where I liked to chain-smoke while he watched the kids, but halfway through decided that Tim did not need this information, so at the last second asserted that I went there "to get gas."

A moment passed.

"Let me get this straight," Tim said in his most annoying voice. "You want your own car so you can drive to the *gas station*? I don't think so."

For days, I slammed around the apartment, rehearsing arguments under my breath. It's true that I didn't like driving in the city, but I could manage certain neighborhoods and surface roads. Tim seldom biked to work anymore, which left me limited to stroller walks with Charles while Tabitha minded Bea. Even when Tim was home, I felt I had to ask permission for the car—I, an adult! At sixteen, I'd had my own car to drive wherever I pleased, for whatever reason, but now I had to submit to an institutional cost-benefit analysis just to leave the house. And since when was Tim more loyal to "the environment" than to his own wife?

Finally, Tim allowed that our family might profit from a second, *used* car.

We hauled the kids to a dealership in a neighboring city. While a mechanic checked out a cheap car I'd found on the Internet, we went to a chain restaurant of the type Tim and I used to mock. They greeted us with open arms, juggling highchairs, crayons, and balloons. Soon we were in a pleather booth with an enormous plate of appetizers, tossing back ranch-drizzled sticks of fried mozzarella. Bea tried the artichoke dip and happily batted her balloon. Charles conducted absorbing experiments on the best way to dip his fry into a pool of ketchup.

"I'm glad we're eating here with our kids," I said without a trace of irony, "instead of all the 'good' places we used to go." Tim nodded agreement while he chewed.

When we got back on the road and passed a cemetery, however, I remarked that it put the nearby shopping district in perspective. When Tim asked what I was talking about, I clarified: "It's good to know that, while we're stuffing our faces with fried food at Applebee's, the dead are looking on in their surpassing wisdom. And sorrow."

"Oh boy," muttered Tim. The discussion turned to my plan to be buried rather than cremated after I died, a prospect Tim found morbid. He opined that I wouldn't want "all sorts of people" trampling on my grave.

I countered that yes, I would, as in death I expected to be more sociable and generally open-minded. "*All* may drink deep from the memory of my life," I quipped, thinking this line would make him laugh.

"I'm drinking from it right now," said Tim flatly, causing me to look at him sideways. "Excuse me if I sneak a nip a little early."

"...Are you saying you *wish* I was dead?"

"No, no. Forget it."

The traffic light turned green and we drove on.

Tim and the mechanic conversed at length, their heads together in the bay, while I occupied Charles and Bea in the fluorescent lobby and watched through a window. They agreed that we probably shouldn't buy the car. Tim explained the mechanic's reasoning to me and we left.

Two hours of billboards and traffic rushed past the passenger-side window, and I silently watched it all go by, hands in my lap. I should have known that I would not be getting a car, that life was not going to normalize in any way. I was on a different trajectory right now, one that could not be stopped by Tim or anyone. This had been made clear a few weeks earlier, though at the time, I'd been reluctant to believe it.

I had been downtown, waiting for Tim outside the newsroom. It was housed in a tall white clock tower whose topmost point pierced the city's skyline. The sunbaked streets, which smelled faintly of trash, seemed seedier and more doomed than usual. A one-legged man dozed, twitching, in his wheelchair; a woman shrieked into her cell phone about "the six hundred dollars in my wallet"; a skinny old man lay sprawled on a blanket on the sidewalk where another man prodded him with his toe, to the bemusement of three passing teenaged boys— one of whom, with exquisite indifference, let slip to the ground a Burger King bag. Girls in flapping flip-flops hauled open-mouthed babies across the street as if weighed down by sacks of grain.

Tim had taken the kids inside for a few minutes, but I had not felt up to workplace introductions. Now, out of the corner of my eye, I caught sight of the tower's pinnacle and startled: There was a figure perched in front of the clock's face, about to jump. Her long hair swirled around her, and she wore a plain silver-gray dress. It was—it couldn't be!—the girl with the baby in the rose garden. Shocked, I looked around for somebody to tell, when she stepped off the ledge and floated down to hover twenty feet or so above the street. She surveyed it thoughtfully, with her palms upturned. I gaped, speechless. The one-legged man awoke, coughing, and stared right at her with a dazed expression, but no one else even looked up. After eight or nine seconds, she simply vanished.

Bursting through the building's front door into the bright afternoon, Tim said, "Sorry that took so long! It's a madhouse in there today."

"Okay," I said numbly, reaching to take one of the children off his hands.

On the long drive home to 3C, I reflected on these events until we were back in the building garage, pulling into our one allotted space. Practically speaking, I couldn't argue with the day's result. Having my own car would be an excess, a hassle, in the city. My shoulders sagged with resignation, the sense that I had no control over my life but could only endure its increasing and incommunicable strangeness. Probably we should start looking at double strollers and leave it at that.

We went upstairs.

OUR APARTMENT WAS LESS THAN 800 SQUARE FEET, AND THOUGH THE kids didn't have much space, I wanted them to have everything else. We had no room for a nursery, so we turned the whole place into a nursery. We bought a short red plastic slide for Charles and set it up in the living room. A child's easel announced his name in chalk (CHARLES!) even though he couldn't read it. Bea had a playmat by the couch made out of big, soft pastel tiles. She had a bouncy chair and something called a Mega Circus Exersaucer, a sort of miniature spaceship that made noise when she jumped up and down. We hauled the crib, now toddler-sized, into the dining room as a playpen. To get into the kitchen, I had to roll it out of the way. Every surface was cluttered with baby books, interlocking blocks, and tubs of finger paint—every surface except Tim's desk, where mounds of Tim's stuff grew and listed.

I barely noticed the mess anymore because Charles and Bea were happy there.

They laughed and smiled all the time: Charles at the top of his red slide beaming with courage, Bea flapping her arms in delight as the toys attached to the Exersaucer whirled and squeaked. They didn't grasp our non-ideal and precarious situation. They did not ask about their missing house, yard, and white picket fence. This was their home, and everything glowed with significance and magic.

Every morning, I made the beds and put on lipstick. I tidied up as best I could throughout the day, trying to make the apartment nice. We'd just keep swimming, like the blue fish in *Finding Nemo*, swimming, swimming…

"KITTY?" CHARLES SAID ONE MORNING IN THE KITCHEN, TUGGING THE knee of my pants.

"What?" I was washing bottles in the sink, scrubbing out remnants of sour milk with a long, narrow brush. "Oh, she's not here anymore."

"*Kitty!*"

"Hey! It's all right." I reached down and ruffled his hair. "We can go visit her anytime. She's just at Tabitha's, remember?"

Charles mulled this over, then said, skeptically, "Who?"

"You know, Tabitha. Downstairs! The white-haired lady. We can't really keep the kitty here, but we can visit her. Don't worry. Hey, hey—" Having lost interest, Charles was reaching up to the counter, eyeing a glass placed tantalizingly close to the edge. I took his hand and redirected it, gently steering him toward the kitchen door.

"Okay, well, bye," he said and disappeared from sight.

To the meditative sound of running water, I wondered how Tabitha's surgery had gone. It was surprising that I hadn't heard from her since then. The days all blended together, and it was easy to lose track of time.

But come to think of it, strangely, I hadn't seen her for weeks.

19

WHAT CAN YOU SAY ABOUT A BABY?

I have a photo of Beatrice at six months, sitting propped against an olive-green pillow. She's wearing a white dress with lavender flowers, facing the camera with a faint, twinkly smile, as in a royal portrait. Six months old and all her qualities were in her face: perspicacity, mirth, sweetness. I did not imagine or wish them into being. They were already there.

She slept next to me every night, using some inexplicable power to bulldoze me to the edge of the bed, like a lima bean moving a mountain. At four a.m. I teetered there, listening to her snore. I called her Minnie the Moocher, but in her nighttime aspect only. Mornings upon waking, she smiled at me as if I were the best, most important person to ever live, and all was forgiven. And forgotten. I liked to put her in a dress with a blue whale on it and watch her play with the matching hat.

Meanwhile Charles was developing a preference for being nude, or nearly nude. Every morning, he insisted that I take off his shirt. And get him a bottle. Then he swaggered around the place, shirtless and drinking like some pint-sized Hef, removing the nipple from his lips only to engage in petty argument. In theory, I wanted my children to form their own opinions, as this would indicate intelligence and perhaps even giftedness. But that was before I found myself debating the respective merits of a Handel motet and "Polly Wolly Doodle" as sung by a bunch of clowns, with someone wearing nothing but a diaper and stroking the couch with a broken hairbrush.

"I'm not going to discuss it any further, Charles."

"But—"

"The answer is no. I said no, and that's the end of it. I'm not going explain myself to you. N.O. No."

"Mew late?"

"That's right. We'll listen to your music later."

"Pah Wah."

"Yes. That's what I just said, Charles."

I felt proud of him, this grubby little person with his own ideas. Already, he would cling to me and run away, swoop in for a smeary lollipop kiss and run away. He was almost a little boy, and I felt proud as he scampered ahead of me over the grass.

But I knew Bea was my last baby, and I wanted to hold onto her.

At first, no one came to Tabitha's door.

I knocked again. Beatrice was in her furry pouch around my chest, and the two of us waited. There was a sound from inside, like a chair being scraped over the floor.

The door opened a crack, and a middle-aged man came into view. He was older than Jeremy, with dark, curly hair and a weathered face. Under bushy eyebrows, his coffee-colored eyes sized me up.

"Yes?"

"Hi. I'm a friend of Tabitha's. Is she home?"

"Are you the one with the cat?"

"Yes." I tried to remember what Tabitha had told me about her older son. He'd lived in Europe for a time, working as a musician-for-hire and cab driver. He had been married to a Swiss woman, but the marriage had broken up. No children.

"My mother's out of town," he said. "I'm Mark. She asked me to keep an eye on things while she was away."

"Oh! That was fast. Did her surgery go all right?"

"Yes, very well," said Mark. He had a low voice, cultured but with some gravel in it. He was an attractive man and barely resembled his brother—half-brother, technically. "I'll tell her you stopped by."

"Okay. Thank you. My name's Cara. I live upstairs—"

But he had already shut the door.

I was halfway up the stairs when I realized I had forgotten to ask where she'd gone.

SOMETHING WAS OFF. SOME SILENT TRAIN ROUNDING A CORNER HAD derailed, and now the cars were piling up, each one crashing into the one before. It was at Tabitha's, or in 3C, or outside in the city. The air shimmered as sparks flew off the thing happening in slow motion.

Where was its center, the main event?

"City Pimps Get Younger," Tim read aloud, frowning down at the front page of his paper. "Now that's a classic headline. Who came up with that?"

"City what?"

"Pimps."

"City pimps do what?"

"Get younger."

"Get younger what?"

"*They're* getting younger."

"The pimps?"

"Yes, the city pimps. The *city's* pimps, it should say. They're not official city pimps."

"So pimps are younger now. In the city."

"Right."

"How old were they before?"

"Like thirty."

"Huh." I spooned a bite of pureed sweet potato into Bea. "Why are they getting younger?"

"Because of the Internet," said Tim, scanning the page. "They're more tech-savvy."

"Oh. Makes sense. Do you think it might one day be possible"— I made a funny face at Bea to hold her interest—"to live in a place where there are no 'city pimps'?"

"What do you have against—"

"Tim, I'm serious. This town is chock-full of degenerates and criminals. We have to get the kids out of here."

"'Degenerates'?"

"City pimps! The complete breakdown of society is just taken for granted here. You have to have money to avoid it, and we don't."

"I think you're being kind of a snob right now," said Tim.

"Oh, please. You don't see it because you're sitting in your office, talking to scientists all day. But I'm out on the street, and I can tell you, people are not *well* here, Tim. It's like the air is poisoned, and we're breathing it."

"What, because there are poor people who don't have a degree in English Lit? And you're afraid their poor people cooties will rub off on our kids? Wow."

"It has nothing to do with poor."

"But you just said—"

"Money helps," I conceded. "It would make raising kids here easier. But it's not the important thing."

"And what is?"

"I don't know. Moral clarity." I had scooped Bea out of her highchair and now balanced her on one outflung hip.

There was an incredulous silence.

"Moral. Clarity."

"That's right. Impressing on them that good and evil are real things. If no one seems to grasp that because they're too busy pimping each other out, pimping *themselves*—"

"I didn't notice a lot of moral clarity when we were dating," Tim said acidly.

"I didn't mean that. Maybe a little. But—"

"What's gotten into you?" snapped Tim. "You sound so reactionary lately, it's like you're not even the same person. What happened?"

"What *happened*?" I jiggled Bea. "What do you mean, 'what happened?' I had two babies, that's what."

"I had them too!"

"Not like I did, you didn't."

He shook his head, and I swept our daughter out of the room.

"OH, JEREMY!" I CALLED FROM THE LAUNDRY ROOM DOOR. HE WAS leaving Tabitha's place and looked up, startled.

"I'm Cara, the neighbor?" I said, loping down the hall toward him. "I was just doing some laundry, and I saw you. Hi."

"Hello," said Jeremy. He turned the key with a soft click and removed it from the locked door.

"How's your mom?"

"Good, thanks. I was watering her plants while she's away."

"Yeah, I was wondering about that. She watches Mew for me—the cat—so I was curious. Where did she go?"

"She's visiting an old school friend back East. They've been planning it for a while."

"How nice! Did she need me to...? I mean, I can check on things. I'm right here. It's no problem."

"Oh no," said Jeremy with a thin smile. "She specifically told me not to bother you. Said you had enough on your hands. I can look after things just fine."

"You and your brother," I said.

"Excuse me?"

"You and Mark. I came by the other day, and he answered the door."

"Yes! Me and Mark. We've got it covered."

"How long is he in town?" I asked pleasantly.

"I'm sorry, but I have to run. It's very nice seeing you again. I'll let Mother know you stopped by!"

"So you talk to her on the phone?" I asked, but he was striding toward the elevator and waved without looking back.

After the elevator door closed, I remained in the hall. Something was off. I raised my fist and knocked softly.

"Tabitha?"

Pressing my ear to the door, I didn't hear a sound. Yet my spine tingled with some old sixth sense, an apprehension of some presence just out of reach.

I'm not like other girls. Maybe my old, naïve boast had contained a kernel of truth. I'd been a solitary child, left to my own devices while my parents worked and some distracted baby-sitter watched TV. Occasionally, I'd felt a mental sensation like a twitch, some fingertip plucking a string inside my mind, and looked around, wonderingly. Was someone there? But I was still alone, surrounded by books in my pastel-colored bedroom or playing house with my dolls under the tree in our front yard.

Yet, I couldn't shake the feeling that I wasn't alone, really. One particular memory stood out: I was six or seven, flying high in the backyard swing, bare legs stretched out before me, body tracing an arc as far as gravity allowed and down again. Over the treetops, in the patch of blue sky my toes seemed to touch just for an instant, someone was there, unseen but watching. I was as certain of this as I was of anything.

"David?" I called out. "Is that you?"

Just like outside Tabitha's door, nobody answered.

DURING THAT YEAR, THE YEAR CHARLES TURNED TWO AND BEA WAS born, the things I did not care about could fill a book. My indifference to the following subjects was infinite: agriculture, astronomy, biology, chemistry, computer science, engineering, geology, law, medicine, oenology, politics, public health, queer theory, Spanish, telemetry, the Uniform Commercial Code, and zoning.

All I cared about was the children's well-being and, in a related matter, my own sanity. This was more than enough to occupy me day and night.

It was, on every level, a lonely job. "The fox sees every little thing," I once said cryptically to Tim, quoting some unknown sage. "The hedgehog sees one big thing."

At night, Beatrice curled behind my curved back, holding a hank of my hair in her fist. Charles slept beside us in his toddler bed, and we sailed through the night together like a single ship: one at the bow, one at the stern, I the vessel and the sail. Nothing could separate me from these children. Bea was behind me, shielded, and I would see everything first. Hold on. I would scan the landscape and relay it back to her. She would not be flying blind, not this one. Not if I could help it.

Who or what told the truth? Books, probably. But not the ones I had been reading lately, filled with one-pot recipes and childcare stratagems. At the library by the lake, browsing the stacks with one hand on the brand-new double stroller, I felt like the old man in *Mr. Sammler's Planet*, who "with his bushy eye took in the books and papers of his West Side bedroom and suspected strongly that they were the wrong books, the wrong papers." Saul Bellow knew a lot, but he didn't know about being a young mother in the city, subject to strange hallucinations she could not explain, aware of presences she couldn't see but felt as distinctly as water from the faucet on her hand. No one had written that book, as far as I knew, yet that was the one I needed.

We drifted, the children and I, down musty rows of Fiction, Psychology, and Religion. Charles wouldn't stay quiet much longer, and Bea would be up from her nap soon. It was a luxury to be at the library, but I had better wrap it up fast.

On a metal cart at the end of an aisle, one large book sat abandoned: *The Encyclopedia of Saints*. I knew very little about Catholic saints except that they tended to be eccentric: Catherine the anorexic, Joan the cross-dresser, Lucy the virgin. There was Little Theresa, the mediocre nun; not to be confused with Big Teresa, the tough-minded mover and shaker. There was Cecilia the child bride, Monica the nagger, Felicity the pregnant slave. Flipping the pages, I recalled how it often went with them: death by fire, by sword, by lion. I'd forgotten, or never learned, the strange things they'd insisted they'd seen: a gold ring on a finger, invisible to all but the wearer; a bronze ladder in the sky; a mysterious "child dressed in white who appeared to be about four or five years old"; a flock of doves that circled the house at an infant's birth and reappeared at key times in her life. An Italian girl, the well-educated daughter of a pharmacist, came to believe that an angel was her constant companion, familiar as a brother. She maintained that he protected her from evil spirits who harassed her for hours on end, one "in the shape of a big black dog" who "put his paws on my shoulders, hurting me."

Charles was growing restless, kicking the front half of the stroller with both legs while Beatrice stirred in the back. It was time to check out, so Religion (200-299, per Dewey) it was. Maybe this book was the right book, or one of them. Ten minutes later, with *The Encyclopedia* and a few more impulse-grab 200s in my bag, we reemerged into the disordered city, its elements unnumbered, unclassified.

"Sorry I'm late," said Tim. "Some of us grabbed drinks after work, and it ran long. I'm surprised you're still up."

I closed my current book, penned by a Frenchwoman named Simone Weil—*Evil being the root of mystery, pain is the root of knowledge*—before she wandered frailly, fatally off the reservation.

"Who's Erin Keller?" I asked mildly.

"Who?" He busied himself placing a little pile of loose change on the table.

"Erin Keller."

"She's a reporter at the paper. Why?"

"Why was her press badge in your pocket?"

Tim's face registered surprise. "I don't follow."

"I was doing the laundry," I said, "and there was something in your pants pocket. A laminated press pass for Erin Keller. Were you at some event with her, or what?"

"Oh, we're doing this fall package," Tim said, matter-of-fact. "I'm pretty sure I mentioned it to you. It's a group project on the city's tech sector. Erin's on the business desk, so we're collaborating on a few pieces. She's very serious about her work."

"The *business* desk?" I tried to wrap my mind around this type of person. "Was she out drinking with you guys tonight?"

"She was, actually."

"And who else?"

"What?" Tim seemed suddenly hard of hearing.

"Who else was there?" I asked sharply.

"Oh, you know. People came and went."

"No, I don't know. Come on, Tim, what is going on? Were you out drinking with this woman?"

"Look, she's become a friend, all right?" Tim said with sudden irritation. "I feel sorry for her. She's been putting in long hours on our project, and it's become an issue with her partner."

"She has a 'partner'?" I repeated. "Oh, how nice. Well, I don't know what that means, Tim, but I do know you have a wife. You have two children. Your life revolves around your work, okay. I knew that when I met you. But you do not get to make decisions that affect me, that affect our kids—"

"No one's making any decisions."

"—while I'm stuck here, cleaning the diaper pail."

"You're stuck here, as you put it," Tim said coldly, "because you want to be stuck here. You used to be a journalist yourself. We had that in common. Now I'm not even sure what to say to you."

"Well, you could start with, 'Honey, I'm home!' Instead of hanging out with Erin discussing business. Tell Erin to mind her *own* business."

Tim muttered something.

"What?"

"Duly noted," he repeated grimly. Something occurred to me, and I gasped.

"What?" Tim demanded.

"'I need to talk to you,'" I recited, my mouth suddenly dry.

"We're talking now."

"No. She sent that e-mail! A few weeks back. 'I need to talk to you.' What was that all about?" My voice had climbed several notes into a shriek.

"You'll wake the kids," Tim hissed.

"I don't care! What are you doing? What's going on? I can't believe it."

"Nothing! I'm not doing anything. Nothing happened. Cara?"

"I'm going to throw up."

"Nothing happened! I'm sorry, okay? I'm sorry I was out so late."

I ran to the bathroom, slammed the door, and retched into the sink.

ALL THROUGH THE NEXT DAY, MY HANDS SHOOK. PLATES CLATTERED noisily into the cabinet, mugs slipped into the sink and cracked. The children seemed to exist on the other side of a screen, muted and distant, as I scraped fingers through my unwashed hair. Around me bobbed a random and incomprehensible array of objects, props of an abandoned script.

"I'll be back in five minutes," I said. The kids were doing their own thing and didn't look up. They had a million toys, a crib, the TV on. The odds were very good they would be fine, and so in one swift decision I played the odds.

Just outside 3C, a fire escape door led to a narrow balcony made of black metal. I lit a cigarette and sat down with my back against the building. The fire escape interested me, as it was four floors up. Its black rails were sun-warmed, but the sidewalk below looked white and cool, the fresh underside of a summer pillow. With one small tap, a crust of ash tumbled into oblivion in silence: a non-event, a nothing.

I dangled my feet off the ledge, rubbing my temples. A ringing sense of isolation frightened me all of a sudden. I knew anxiety, but this was of a different order. I desperately needed to tell someone what was going on: in my brain, in 3C, with Tim. I needed to ask someone where Tabitha could be. I needed them to explain why the train wreck taking place was my own life, when I had followed the most well-worn path on earth: marriage and children. Tracing and retracing my steps, I couldn't name the first mistake. I didn't know anything, and I was alone.

20

Fast-acting nicotine calmed me enough to get back to the grind. I stubbed out my cigarette and rejoined the children in 3C. The odds had played out in my favor; no one had choked or drowned or set the place on fire or banged a two-inch gash in their head. I was doing a lousy job today, and yet I had been spared.

"Mom?"

"Not now, Charles."

I took the phone into the bedroom and thought hard. I had a fleeting urge to call Gemma but decided against it. Gemma was busy entertaining herself and found my life vaguely pathetic. Was *Gemma* making the right choices? I wondered. I'd begun to think of her as dull, but maybe she was playing a long game I didn't understand.

I dialed.

"Hello?"

"Hi, Mom. It's me."

"Oh, Cara!" Claudia sounded surprised.

"I just thought I'd call. It's been awhile, so."

"Well, it's so nice to hear your voice! How are the kiddos?"

"Good."

"How's Tim?"

"He's fine," I said reflexively.

"Work going well?"

"I guess so. Busy. You know how it is."

"Oh yes. The life of a reporter! And how are things with you?"

"Uh, they're okay. I'm kind of tired today. It's been a rough week."

"I'll bet it has," Claudia said gaily. "Those kids are probably running you ragged!"

"No, it's not that. The kids are fine. It's just…"

"Is everything all right?" asked Claudia after an awkward silence.

"Tim's… Tim has this friend at work. This woman. They're working together on this project, and they… She e-mails these weird messages. He says it's nothing, but…" Here I started to cry. "I'm just so tired, Mom. I don't know what to think."

"Oh no. I'm sorry you're upset. It's probably nothing."

"They went out to a bar. I asked him about it, but I feel like he's not telling the truth, like I'm being *managed*."

"I can't see Tim being unfaithful," Claudia mused aloud. "He's so devoted to you and the kids. Are you sure you're not reading too much into a work relationship?"

"I don't know. He said we don't have anything to talk about anymore. That I was more interesting when I worked."

"Well, have you thought about going back to work?"

"…What?"

"I'm just saying, I think it's hard on Tim to be the sole breadwinner for so long. He has a very stressful job, and—"

"You're worried about *Tim*?"

"I'm not taking sides," Claudia said. "I just think Tim's doing the best he can under the circumstances. As are you! It's a difficult situation all around."

"The kids are still so young. Bea's not even one. There's plenty of time to work, but right now I feel like they need me here."

"When you were little, we had a girl come watch you. Cindy, I think her name was? You probably don't remember. She played with you and read you books."

"Mom, you and Dad were professors. You were home all the time, had every summer off, four weeks at Christmas. Most jobs aren't like that. I would be putting them in day care nine hours a day, five days a week."

"Could you have a baby-sitter watch them at home?"

"You mean, could we hire a full-time nanny? We can't afford that. Are you kidding?"

"Could you maybe go part time?"

"Mom, that's not the point. I think Tim's having an emotional affair. It could be a real affair, for all I know. Though I'd be surprised if he had the energy."

"What's an emotional affair?"

"Oh, come on. Are you telling me you don't have any idea—"

"No, no. I think I understand. He's made a friend at work, a female friend. And you feel neglected. Is that right?"

"No. That's—you make it sound like—no. Just never mind."

"Well, I'm trying to understand. Don't be like that."

"You're not trying to understand. You're trying to put it in a box that's simple for *you*, easy for *you*. You have no idea what my life is like. You never call, you never ask if I'm okay. You ask how Tim's doing, or what size Charles wears, or what the weather's like—"

"Because I don't want to bother you! I know you're busy, and the kids may be down for a nap. I don't want to pry into your life. It's none of my business."

"None of your *business*? I'm your daughter. If Bea were in this kind of mess, I'd be calling her every day."

"What kind of mess? What are you talking about?"

"This. Everything. I can't go on like this, Mom. I'm falling apart. I need some kind of help or therapy or I don't know what. And you're telling me to go back to *work*? 'Oh, just hire a nanny.' Unbelievable." I ended with a string of obscenities, something about her being Mother of the Year.

A moment of silence on her end of the line.

"There's no need for that." The cheery overtone to Claudia's voice was gone, and with it some paper-thin version of her, some habitual brave front. "I've done my best," she said in this new voice, at once brittle and aged. "You're an adult, Cara, and life is very hard."

"I know it's hard." I sounded about eight years old. "What should I do?"

"I don't know," Claudia said in an odd tone, as if mulling a riddle of pure philosophy. "I don't know." Her pitch rose at the end; it was almost a question. "Ever since David died…"

I listened closely, since this period included my whole life.

"...I haven't really cared about anything."

I was silent for a long moment. Dimly, I sensed that she was giving me a gift: telling me, in my hour of desperation, the hard truth I needed to hear. This was the key that unlocked everything: the agoraphobia, the vertigo, the nausea brought on by too much empty space, by too much nothingness. The fear that the void could swallow me at any time. Claudia was handing me crucial information, which some part of me squirreled away.

But in that moment, I felt rage. For a few seconds, I couldn't speak. Finally, my manners kicked in. I was, in many ways, a well-raised child.

"I'm sorry to hear that, Mom," I said.

Claudia seemed to like this answer. It was possible she was desperate for sympathy. Her plight had lasted a long time.

The conversation trailed off, and I said I'd better go check on Charles.

ON SOME LEVEL, I ALWAYS KNEW THAT MY MOTHER BELIEVED IN nothing. As I grew up, there had been a hole at the center of our lives, a hole that sometimes seemed like merely an illusion or a dark mood. We shopped for clothes, we went to dinner, we laughed at sitcoms on TV. But beneath these carefree moments, I was aware of being inches from freefall: out on an invisible ledge with Claudia, a ledge she never left. We didn't discuss it, and I instinctively knew not to look down.

Who could let her nineteen-month-old child go to bed with a fever, not realizing how high it was or that the medicine drops would wear off? Who could sleep through the night in the next room while he, at some point, slipped into unconsciousness? Anyone could. Claudia had, and it was just a dumb mistake. A rookie error. Her firstborn had suffered a massive seizure and, by noon the next day, he was gone.

After that, what? Only the circus of human ephemera: an eccentric collection of masks, totems, altars, ceremonial garb, pottery, weapons, and tools. A grab-bag to riffle through for some vague educative purpose or just to pass the time. Claudia taught this stuff every year; she knew it all: the gods and customs of the Yanomamo, the Mi'kmaq, the Maori, the Igbo. But she did not know where her child was, or why he was no longer with her. There was no reason, none at all, but the smiling boy who had only just been in her arms existed nowhere now. The prairie night sky was a bowl of distant stars, and her child was not among them, or beyond them. He was even further than that.

Having a second child didn't heal or unbreak her. She was just going through the motions: doing her best and running out the clock.

OUTSIDE THE SIX WINDOWS OF OUR LIVING ROOM, THE SKY WAS AN innocent expanse of pink and blue: nursery colors. The cloud-filled sky was telling a children's story, but the moon would tell the real one, haunting and lunatic, the orbit of a pale body through an infinity of darkness. Still unable to focus on housework or the kids, I spent the rest of the day waiting for the moon, feeling trapped in these rooms—in the city—like an animal in a cage. Only the moon saw and understood me. The moon had my back.

I had made a mistake, or several mistakes. That much was certain.

For hours, I sat in bed with my head in my hands and tried to sort it out. I had ushered two children into the disaster of modern life, or maybe just life, period. I could not fix it, but only compound the error: by hauling myself across the city to work; by keeping us stuck in a tiny, cramped apartment; by flying the three of us back to Claudia's for an indefinite visit; by confronting Tim or by looking the other way. Something was wrong here—*people were not well*—and the poison was seeping into 3C. It was seeping into me.

Dimly, I realized I should not be around the children.

Tim came home, and I said I was going to bed. Just that. I had no instructions or advice, no reports or notable moments to share. People had clocked out of fast food shifts with more fanfare than I handed off my two kids—not even physically touching them, just a gesture in their direction. I re-entered our single bedroom, closed the door, and locked it.

"Uh…"

"Good night!"

Even so, I could barely sleep for dreams, weird and twisting into each other like the strands of a rope in which I turned and thrashed. I dreamed my father had been buried under what was now an empty parking lot. Walking by it on the sidewalk, it upset me to think that he was under there: paved over and forgotten. I puzzled over how to get him out, but realized it was hopeless. Then I was in the spare bedroom of my mother's house when the closet door opened and he was in there on a stepladder, with his back to me, getting down the Christmas lights. I closed my eyes because I knew it wasn't really him, just an apparition that was...tormenting me? That was probably the right word, because I felt so terrible about the parking lot. I opened the bedroom door to leave, and he was before me in the hall, opening his arms for a hug. But because I knew it wasn't him, just a trick of my own mind, he transformed into someone else, a stranger with gray bristles on his face.

In the gray light of early morning, I got out of bed and went to the window.

Looking out, I saw something very surprising.

"I got your message," said Janine over the phone the next morning. "How are you doing today?"

Hearing her voice, I vaguely regretted that I'd called her after my talk with Claudia. On one hand, it was nice to hear someone inquire about my well-being. On the other hand, I had spent six therapy sessions with Janine while pregnant with Bea, sessions in which I had alternately felt embarrassed, bored, misunderstood, and tetchy. I had no reason to think today would be any different.

"Better," I said.

"I'm glad to hear that. In your voicemail yesterday, you sounded distressed. Is everything all right?"

"Um. I don't know how to... Yeah, I guess."

"Are you in any physical danger?"

"No."

"Are you having any thoughts about harming yourself?"

"No. Nothing like that." There was the briefest of silences. "I mean…"

"Go on."

"I just mean, obviously there are possibilities. Anyone could see that. It's impossible not to notice."

"Notice what?"

"Well, there's the fire escape balcony, for one thing. Obviously it would be possible—not that anyone would ever do this—to hang yourself off it. With a belt or whatever. Or just jump off! It probably wouldn't kill you. It's not that high up. Obviously that would be the quickest, but it's risky."

"Okay," said Janine, whose voice had somehow become even calmer. "And what else have you been noticing?"

"Well, the apartment is full of…objects. Anyone with little kids is constantly aware of that. It's baby-proofed, but it's not people-proofed. Do you get what I'm saying? It's full of razors, knives, sharp scissors. It's quite amazing, when you look around. Who *lives* like this?" I heard myself laugh unconvincingly.

"Cara," said Janine, so very calm, as if gazing at me over big sunglasses and an umbrella drink without a care in the world, just one friend chatting with another. "I think it would be a good idea for you to come in today."

"Okay," I heard myself agreeing.

"Are you with the children right now?"

"Yes."

"Is there someone you can leave them with?"

"You mean, like right now? No. My husband won't be home till six or seven."

"Here's what we're going to do," Janine said pleasantly, sipping her imaginary strawberry drink. "I'd like you to put the children in the car—"

"Tim's got the car."

"You don't have a car?"

"No."

"Then I'll come to your house," she said brightly after a pause. "Where do you live?"

IT IS ABSURD TO BE IN AN AMBULANCE WHEN YOU ARE PERFECTLY capable of driving yourself to the hospital. Not that I could drive, because I hated city driving and the hospital was downtown at a tricky intersection with too many lanes, but Tim could drive. At the moment, though, Tim had his hands full: Bea in his arms and Charles on his shoulders. The three of them formed a stupefied tableau on the curb while two EMTs hoisted me into the ambulance backward in a little chair. I gazed out solemnly at Tim and the kids like an icon being paraded through the streets of some crowded and pious country.

This was too bad, and I was sorry, but it was probably for the best.

It was an emergency hold, and we were lucky someplace had an open bed. Someplace not terrible—Janine had seemed surprised, like I had beat tough odds. The place was pretty nice, as these things go.

"Say bye-bye, Charles," I instructed, waving my hand. "Bye-bye. I'll be back soon. Don't worry! I'll be—"

The back doors closed and, after a minute or so, the engine started. There was no need to use the siren. This wasn't TV. Like a ship, the ambulance eased into motion and down the road.

Settling in for a peaceful ride, I recalled the day. It had taken an odd turn, but it had started quietly...

Suddenly it occurred to me: the meaning of what I had seen out the window. And then I knew I had to get back right away.

21

Day 12

I've been at Mildred W. almost two weeks: long, spacey days disconnected from the outside world. The yellow pages stacked on my desk are covered with jagged script. I feel rested and clear-headed, and I have pressing tasks at home—things no one else would understand, let alone do.

So, it's time to talk my way out, to ace my psychological assessment this afternoon. No more nattering on about the city or the movies. I must sell the idea that I was just a frazzled mom who overreacted to a marital spat. Since then, I've had a chance to rest, get some perspective. I now have pills to keep me on an even keel, like the millions of other American women on psych meds—one in four, by some counts! I'm ready to be released into the wild.

I've spent hours thinking about how a sane modern mother is supposed to sound: brimming with informed and up-to-date concerns, straight out of a women's magazine or morning talk show. The more bland and trivial my conversation, the more reassuringly normal I will seem. So, the next interview should go something like this:

A: I'm doing much better, and I'm ready to go home. I miss the kids.

Q: I'm sure your children are in good hands, Mrs. Nielsen. The important thing is to make sure you're stable and well before we send you back. How are you feeling?

A: I feel preoccupied, to tell you the truth.

Q: Oh?

A: Charles, my son, has a Well Child appointment in three days, and I'd really like to be there because I have some questions for the pediatrician.

Q: Questions like what?

A: When he eats eggs, his stools are watery, I've noticed. I'm not sure whether I can give him peanuts or soy—mostly peanuts, because it would be nice to give him peanut butter crackers, but what if he's allergic? I'm wondering if there's some kind of test besides, you know, giving him peanuts. Also, at his twelve-month appointment, his growth chart said he was in the 75th percentile for height—

Q: That's very good!

A: Yes, we were pleased. His father's tall. But at eighteen months, the graph dipped down to only 62 percent! The doctor said it was no big deal and would probably self-correct, but I'm wondering if maybe it's his diet? I want him to attain his full potential height. Also, my daughter—

Q: Sorry to interrupt. How old is she again?

A: Six months. She isn't even on a day care list. The time has just flown by!

Q: Are you thinking about going to back to work?

A: Yes. We need the money. And to be honest, I'm a bit...

Q: Go on.

A: Bored at home, I guess you'd say? So, I need to start looking into that, and of course the question is what day care can she still get into at this point, or do we try find an affordable nanny, maybe a nanny share? All of them have their pros and cons, but I think if we could find a bilingual nanny, that would be best. I feel like Spanish or Chinese would be very useful for Charles.

Q: And are you still breastfeeding, Mrs. Nielsen?

A: Yes, I am. Or at least, I was, before I left. My husband's had to give her formula, and I'm worried she'll never go back. If we switch her over too early, it could affect her immune system, her I.Q., who knows what else? It seems so unfair that she could fall behind developmentally, just because I—

Q: Don't upset yourself, Mrs. Nielsen. I think we can get you home soon.

In fact, it's frightening what I have to go home to, but I don't think of that. There isn't much time left. So, I rehearse this conversation in my mind and practice my facial expressions, drumming my fingers on the chair.

"Hey. Going somewhere?"

Walking down the hall, I paused before an open door that led into a patient's room, identical to mine. Flee was inside, packing some clothes into a tote bag on the bed.

"Yeah. I'm checking out," she replied.

"Wow. Good for you. Did the doctor clear you today?"

"He didn't need to," said Flee. "I signed myself in. Now I'm signing myself out. After so many episodes, I've learned when I need a break."

I didn't know how to respond. She still looked vulnerable and young, as if a strong wind would knock her over. But so did most of the young women toughing out life in the city. "I hope I won't be far behind," I said. "I'm ready to get out of here. I miss my kids."

"Do you feel different?" Flee asked. "Compared to when you arrived, I mean."

"I do. I don't know whether it's the pills, the sleep, or all the hours of peace and quiet. Maybe all three. I guess I needed a timeout from life."

Flee cocked her head, a roll of black socks in one hand. The merest hint of a smile twitched her lips, as if she didn't quite buy my explanation.

"Father Ray said a funny thing," she remarked.

"Oh?"

"He said maybe I wasn't here so much for me. He said that, maybe, this time, I was here for you."

My mouth fell open. "I don't know why he would say that."

"Oh, come on, Cara. What are you not telling them?" she demanded. "Something important, right? You might as well 'fess up before you leave. It's only me."

"Can I come in?" I asked after a moment. When she nodded, I closed the door behind me and sat down next to her bag on the narrow bed.

"After my son Charles was born…" I began. I told her about the woman in the rose garden, the face the birds drew in the sky. The disappearing curtain made of ants. The way the woman reappeared and floated down from a high tower. Amid these visions, the city pulsated and fizzed, electric with menace. Blocks crammed with human beings and their half-dark hearts, and some days I could feel every one as I gripped the stroller with white knuckles and pushed the children through the crowd.

"It's like having a superpower, but not one I want," I said. "I wish I were making these things up, but I'm not."

"So, Father Ray was right," said Flee after a thoughtful pause.

"Really? How?"

She tossed the socks into the bag and zipped it up, ready to go.

"I'm here to tell you, you're not crazy. I believe you."

A lengthy silence followed.

"Cara? Are you okay?… Are you *crying*?"

"No. I'm okay," I said, wiping my nose with my hand like a child. "Finally. Thank you. That's what I needed to hear. Now I can go home."

22

AT THE END OF THE FOURTH CENTURY IN NORTH AFRICA, A MIDDLE-aged priest wrote, "What should be clear and obvious by now…"

Years after my stint at Mildred W., I'm sitting at a different desk, adding new pages to my old hospital notes in order to finish the story, or one story. Outside the window is green grass, a fence: sights so familiar I barely see them anymore. With my glasses perched in my hair—I'm nearsighted and don't require them for close work—I hold my pen above the page and try to sink into the memory-sensation of those days. Long-ago thought patterns and feelings radiate out to my fingertips, and I physically inhabit them again.

"What should be clear and obvious by now," wrote Augustine, "is that we cannot properly say that the future or the past exists, or that there are three times: past, present, and future. Perhaps we can say that there are three *tenses*"—he liked to use exacting language—"but that they are the present of the past, the present of the present, and the present of the future."

The real past is lost, is what he's saying. That's clear and obvious by now: the past is lost, if it in fact ever existed. My children must have been two and six months old, and Tim and I must have lived in an old, elegant building by the lake, and I must have gone to the hospital and left them standing on the curb. We have the records somewhere, and there is no other plausible account. Yet as I sit here, it all has the flickering quality of a dream, or of a movie watched once in a darkened theater. I must have ended up here somehow, yet I have the innocent sensation of having just been dropped out of the sky. Am I responsible for the vivid and pressing circumstances in which I now find myself? Is Tim? Is someone else?

What happened?

"Here I labor at hard material, Lord," wrote Augustine, "and I am that material. I am a terrain of trouble, worked with much sweat of my brow." Augustine considered man's forgetting (*oblivio*) a mystery in its own right. He often mulled the moral and existential implications of absence. The lack of ability to remember one's own past related to the lack of being (*defectus entis*) that, to him, defined evil.

Augustine would say it is important to sift through events and try to take responsibility for your part. To try to grasp and appreciate what you've done. To try to understand, as best you can, what happened.

CHARLES! BEATRICE!

My children seemed to have aged months in just twelve days. Golden-haired Charles seemed self-possessed, even debonair: the newfound confidence of a boy who had gone two weeks without his mother and survived just fine. He chattered happily as I clung to him in a teary hug.

Bea seemed even smarter and more alert, if possible. Her grey-blue-brown eyes took in everything; her smile was the Mona Lisa's. Not for the first time, she gave the impression of someone in the process of forgetting more than I would ever know. She was not limited by language and logic yet, not in the linear world with us but still polysensory, pansophical. Her diaper was heavy, I noticed: a minor oversight by Tim. But never mind!

"Welcome home, honey," Tim said, hugging me. He seemed humbled and exhausted. Like a star, I had winked out of existence with no warning, precipitating a crisis. In a flurry of H.R. paperwork, he had wangled several days off and tried to cope.

I cried through lunch, grateful to be back with my own kids who would not eat or sit still and threw half their food on the floor; how I had missed them! Afterward, Tim and I convened in the kitchen for a private chat. He wanted to know all about the hospital, but I waved off this subject, impatient.

"It was fine. Restful. I met some interesting people. The thing is, Tim, before I left, I saw Mew out the bedroom window."

"Mew?" Tim seemed surprised at this turn in the conversation. "You mean, our cat? I thought she was supposed to be with Tabitha."

"Exactly! She *is* supposed to be with Tabitha, and I haven't seen Tabitha in weeks. When I last saw her, she was going to have surgery on her foot. Ever since then, whenever I run into her sons in the hall, they say she's travelling. Does that make sense to you?"

"Her sons? What are they doing here?"

"You see?" I said. "They say they're 'watering her plants' and things like that. They won't let me see into her apartment. But why are they always here? She doesn't have that many plants."

"What does this have to do with Mew?"

"Tabitha knows Mew is an indoor cat," I reasoned, like a prosecutor leading a witness who has no grasp of the big picture. "She was very careful about keeping the windows open just a few inches so Mew couldn't fall or jump out. She'd never let her run out the door. She was a *conscientious* cat owner. I don't think she'd go on a long trip without telling me, because she'd want me to know somebody was taking care of Mew. She might even give Mew back for a few weeks, which would be fine! But none of that happened," I said. "I think those boys of hers are careless. What do they care about a cat?"

"You think they let Mew out?"

"Not on purpose. And if she got out, they're not going to tell me, because I'd immediately be suspicious. *More* suspicious. But I saw her! At first I didn't realize it was her. It was just a little white head in the grass. I thought maybe it was a rabbit. But then I saw her big white tail, like she had jumped. I really think it was her, Tim."

Tim rubbed his eyes with both palms. His wife was fresh out of the psych ward and obsessed with a lost cat. The bustling, purposeful newsroom likely seemed very far away.

"Should I go look for her?" he asked in a doomed voice.

"Yes, definitely. You do that. I'll deal with the Tabitha problem."

"Deal with it how?"

"Ask me no questions…"

"And I'll tell you no lies," Tim finished. "Great. Okay then."

"Daaaa-daaa!" Charles screamed from the next room.

"I'll be right there!" yelled Tim.

"It's nice that he calls you now," I said, and turned to do the dishes. It was good to be home.

BY NOW, IT WAS CLEAR AND OBVIOUS THAT TIM WAS NOT GOING TO tell me the truth about Erin, whatever it was. I had proven myself unqualified; I could not handle the truth. Rattled by my hospitalization, Tim had entered into a placatory mode. He wanted to keep me calm at whatever cost, and this was fine. I had been having a few secret thoughts myself.

The doctors only sent me home after a sober talking-to. I was officially depressed, and I had a refillable prescription for antidepressants. I had been losing it twelve days ago, no question, but now I was focused and steady, like the searching beam of a lighthouse. The pills would not fully kick in for two more weeks, but whatever their effect, I had to keep my mind over the lip of the drug-induced calm, over its topmost edge. Before the medication blunted my intuition, before my mood became cheerful and upbeat, before I didn't see shadows in every corner, I had to act. Because again, no question: the shadows were there.

After twelve days tracing the arc of my relationship with Tim, I felt a certain distance from my marriage, a certain perspective. Today, he seemed not so much a husband as a strategic ally. Tim and I were like two nations with different cultures and a long history of skirmishes rooted in mutual incomprehension. I didn't really understand Tim's country, nor he mine, but our shared life was a series of space-alien invasions and we required each other's tactical aid. Up to a certain point, I could count on Tim, and he could count on me. That was something.

For twelve days, I had watched the orange butterflies outside my window, trying to figure out what they were telling me, why there were never two or four but always three. Was I the missing one and the three butterflies Tim and the kids? Was Bea or Charles missing? Impossible. I'd never let that happen. And gradually it began to dawn on me that maybe the missing one was Tim, that I was gazing out the window on my own future.

"THE CITY ITSELF LIVES ON ITS OWN MYTH," SAID ANOTHER PRIEST, this one writing from a shed in Kentucky in the mid-twentieth century. He had retreated to the shed after some years in Greenwich Village in Manhattan. City people, Thomas Merton wrote, "prefer a stubborn and fabricated dream; they do not care to be a part of the night, or to be merely of the world. They have constructed a world outside the world, against the world."

Tim, the children, and I sat on a blanket by the lake: a family outing to celebrate my return. Everyone but Bea had their own cup of Italian gelato, and the sun was setting. One thing I liked about the city was how every possible kind of person walked around the lake. If you just sat there long enough, you would see everyone: sinewy joggers plugged into their music, office workers on lunch break, pretty girls in tattoos and nose rings, elderly couples pausing to inspect a wildflower or a heron, and mothers—always mothers, singly or in twos or threes, pushing their strollers. Whole families of the foreign-born took in the sights in their colorful clothes and sandals. People in wheelchairs rolled by while their walking friends kept pace. They were all different from me, but not so different in their expressions, which covered the familiar range of human moods.

"I want to get away from the kids this weekend," an African-American woman in braids remarked to her friend as they passed us.

"I don't blame you! You deserve a *break.*"

Watching them all go by, I experienced a respite from all my worries, even about Tabitha. I felt momentarily calm, maybe because Tim was there with me. In fact, we were all there: all present and accounted for. Father, mother, son, and daughter. The thing that little girls imagined while reading their storybooks and tending their baby dolls, we had done. We were still here together, taking in the view, and the city had not destroyed us. Not yet.

"We live in a society that tries to keep us dazzled with euphoria in a bright cloud of lively and joy-loving slogans," groused the priest, who was considered something of a crank even by other priests. "Yet nothing is more empty and more dead, nothing is more insultingly insincere and destructive than the vapid grins on the billboards and the moron beatitudes in the magazines which assure us that we are all in bliss right now."

My children were born in the city, in a hulking Soviet-style hospital that loomed over the freeway. They had unlovely births, as births go: carved out of their freaked-out mother in an operating room by strangers. Their father's newspaper was filled with hideous daily events: people killing and assaulting one another, corruption and incompetence at every turn. It was a mess, the world they'd entered, yet the last rays of sunlight glinting off the lake were somehow magical.

Bea sitting in my lap and Charles in his dad's, twirling his spoon, I had the strange sense that our family was immortal and significant. We seemed at that moment to be the city's beating heart. Tim and I had fallen in love and created two incandescent children, a feat nothing and nobody could take away. A fact time itself could not alter.

It was true, what people said of us: We were a beautiful family.

23

How to conceal a baby monitor in a potted plant?
There was a dusty rubber tree at the end of the second-floor hall.
I didn't have a baby monitor—the apartment was too small to need
one—but they were easy to come by. I wanted to see who was coming
and going from Tabitha's, and at what times. It would be simple to
surveil her door from the rubber-tree pot, but how to disguise the
camera? If Mark or Jeremy discovered it, it would be awkward—or
worse, they might call the police. I considered taping a monitor to
the hall ceiling or the laundry room doorframe. I considered leaving a
teddy bear in the hall with cameras for eyes. None of this was foolproof,
however, so I would have to do it like I did every other job: in person.

"I'm going down to the laundry room," I told Tim. "I'll be back in
a couple hours. I'll take Bea."

"Aren't you going to take the laundry?"

"Nope."

"Are you feeling all right?" he asked carefully from the couch,
where he sat reading a storybook about brave firemen to Charles.

"Yup. See you later. On second thought, I'll take the laundry
basket. That gives me some excuse to be there. Bye!"

I enjoyed my two days in the laundry room. Charles was happy
to zoom his wooden cars along the smooth cement. Sometimes he
played in the industrial-sized sink. Bea didn't care. Each time I heard
the elevator stop at the second floor, I casually moved to the propped-
open door to see who walked by. Emma after school, a punishing tote
bag slung over her shoulder. Brighton in a summer coat, dry cleaning
in one hand and takeout in the other. Sometimes people came up the
stairs: Lachlan Keene, back from a run and checking his pulse with two
fingers. The Missionaries, whose names we still did not know, herding
their neat and quiet children down the hall. I sat in an abandoned
chair, patiently manning my post, waiting for information that would
arrive in its own time.

"Are you spying on Tabitha's sons?" Tim wanted to know the second night.

"Not really. I'm just hanging out."

"Cara. Are you staking out Tabitha's? Because this looks like a stakeout."

"I wouldn't call it… Well, someone needs to do it, Tim! A woman just disappears, and the whole building acts like nothing happened? Everyone's willing to assume she set the cat free and took off without a word? I don't buy it, so yes, I'm 'staking out' her apartment."

"Well, what's going on over there?" asked Tim. "Did you find out anything good?" I suddenly felt glad I'd married a reporter.

"It's hard to say. Mark comes by in the morning around ten. One day he had a bag from the drugstore; the next day, nothing. He was dressed casually in jeans and left midafternoon both days. Jeremy showed up around five-thirty. It looked like he'd come straight from work. The first day he stayed for an hour, and the next, about twenty minutes. He seems in a hurry to leave. I just saw his face for a second and he looked…"

Tim waited.

"Unhappy," I said.

"Have you tried calling Tabitha?" asked Tim.

"It goes to voicemail. Did you have any luck with Mew?"

"No. She could be anywhere by now. I'm sorry, Cara."

"It's okay. I'm not worried about her, for some reason."

"And why is that?"

I thought about it and replied, "She's tougher than she looks."

I WOULD HAVE STAYED DOWN THERE ANOTHER DAY, BUT TIM HAD TO go back to work.

That morning, I stood in the galley kitchen ritually assembling a sandwich, in a trance of significance. The making of the sandwich conjured a certain reality into being. Mayonnaise on one slice. Tim was my husband. Mustard on the other. We were married. Three, no, four slices of ham. We had two children. Swiss cheese. We were nice people. Thin-sliced tomato. Nice people did not betray each other.

Salt. We could be trusted. Pepper. Tim could be trusted. Diagonal slice with a serrated blade. Anger, deep anger, was possible, but it would not be necessary. Frilled toothpicks through each acute triangle. I was an excellent wife!

"I packed your lunch." I handed him a piece of Tupperware with a red lid.

"You did?" Tim seemed surprised. "Thanks. You didn't have to do that."

"I wanted to." My eyes searched his for some sign of where to stake my flag this morning: being a loving wife to Tim; expecting the worst from him; crumbling in devastation at all he had done and would do, given the chance; or not really caring about Tim. He seemed vaguely nervous. I didn't know why.

Now he took me by the shoulders and asked, "Are you going to be all right today?"

I nodded.

"I have a ton to do at work. But if you need anything, call me."

"Yep," I said, relinquishing him to the door, back to work, back to Erin.

"Take it easy, champ," Tim said to Charles, and left.

I LATER LEARNED THERE HAD BEEN RUMORS FLYING AROUND THE newsroom for weeks. Tim never mentioned them, probably because I seemed nervous and fragile enough as it was. He had become an adept at compartmentalization, acting one way at work and trying to fit himself into another shape—a husband and father of small children—at home.

Maybe I hadn't been such an excellent wife. During those years, I was sunk deep in my own thoughts and prone to failures of sympathy, deficits of imagination, for anyone who was not me or the kids. Tim had landed his dream job and was trying to do it well, but his life too must have been shot through with perplexing disappointments. Other colleagues had practical wives who dropped the kids at day care, worked five days a week, and went out for beers with the gang on Fridays. They baked cookies and worked out at the gym. Their mothers lived nearby and helped out. They made it work. The kids were fine. These wives had gotten with the program; they enjoyed the city and accepted its trade-offs like adults.

Meanwhile, Tim's wife was a basket case. She didn't drive, she barely cooked. She didn't want to get a job. She wanted to leave the city, period. She didn't want to take Pilates. She was preoccupied with dark, mysterious themes. What could you do with a wife like that?

Oh yeah: She had also gone crazy for two weeks. They'd let her out, and now she was back home, with you.

Maybe I had blamed Tim for being merely normal, for fitting into the city as snugly as a peg in a pegboard. All he wanted was to be a coffee afficionado on a low-carb diet, pull on his Spandex shorts and ride his $1,400 bike, and generally be a Cool Dad with a cool job. This kind of life—richly symbolic of intelligence, drive, and taste—was to him the ultimate prize, the future we were raising the kids *for*.

But I was different. Another world wanted to talk to me, was always tugging at me for attention. It was weirder than this world and not quite of it. It wanted different things of me than a paycheck, a size six figure, and smooth, ageless skin. It wanted more for my children than robust health and admission to prestigious colleges. This other world insisted it could be trusted, and that the other one was a sham and a bore. I had a foot in each: the mundane and the numinous, the intertwined domains—as Weil might say—of gravity and grace.

The phone rang late that afternoon.

"Well," said Tim in an odd tone I couldn't place. "It's finally happened."

"What?" I was staring down the barrel of someone's anus with a poo-clotted wipe in one hand and a cell phone in the other, and I was in no mood to be trifled with. "What are you talking about? What happened?"

"New management. They offered buyouts to sixteen of us. Sixteen! In editorial alone." He named a sum in the low five figures and then explained that's how much the newspaper would pay him—to quit.

"Oh my gosh," I said, trying to contain my dawning elation. "I'm so sorry! That's—wait, I'm just putting a diaper—that's awful news. So, uh, are you going to take it?"

"What choice do I have?" said Tim, echoing word-for-word my inner monologue of the past two years. What choice, indeed? Was it possible we could finally move?

"Well, we should talk about it," I said diplomatically, as if there could be any doubt as to my own views on the matter.

"Yeah," he said shortly. I had long been the enemy of his city job, and we both knew it. "Look, I hate to do this to you after, you know. It's your first day alone with the kids. But we're all angry and upset, and everyone's going for drinks. It's the end of the paper as we know it. So, if it's okay with you—"

"Go. Absolutely, go. We'll be fine."

"Okay. Thanks, Cara."

What could I say? I knew he'd spend the next hours commiserating with Erin and the gang, the entire newsroom trauma-bonding and remembering old times. Who knew him best? Who did he want to be around at this low moment? Maybe Erin. Probably Erin.

It was the truth, and as I lay the phone down and began to weep, I felt I could handle it after all.

"Mama?"

"It's all right, Charles. It's okay. We're going to move to a new house! You'll have your own room, maybe even a backyard. We'll get you a swing set, like at the park. But just for you and Bea. Daddy's going to find a new job, and…"

"You sad?"

"No, not at all!… Well, I'm a little sad, Charles. It's sad when things end. Now run along, you're all clean. Yay!"

THINGS WERE MOVING FAST.

It was now going to be Tim's turn to unravel, my turn to hold down the fort. Tim would soon be jobless and flailing, and I would be chemically altered, undepressed. We were going to have to heave ourselves into a new life, trailing the kids and all their gear, and it was going to be exhausting. We were going to have to cowboy up and do it as a team.

But first things first.

The next day, I hired a baby-sitter to watch Charles. Bea was coming with me, a necessary party to the plan. I wasn't thrilled about this—making my six-month-old an accessory to a crime while being literally worn around my neck—but there was no other way to do it. I needed a distraction, a red herring. It was all for the greater good. So she was coming.

At three p.m., I was dressed in sweatpants, a stained T-shirt, and slippers, jiggling Bea in her pouch. When the locksmith showed up, I met him at the building door and swung it open.

"Thanks so much. I'm sorry to freak out on the phone. It's just—"

"No worries, ma'am. So, you don't have the key, correct?"

"It's in my purse, inside," I blubbered. "I just ran down to check the mail. I thought I left the door unlocked! My husband's out of town, and when I called him, he reminded me I was supposed to give the baby her medicine at two o'clock! I completely forgot. I just lost track of time."

"Does she have a cold or something?" the locksmith asked as we stepped into the elevator.

"No. I wish. It's special eye drops. She has a virus in her eyes, and if we don't keep them medicated, they'll get even more infected. She could go blind."

"Wow, I'm sorry to hear that."

"It's okay." The door slid open to the second floor. "It's right down here. I feel so stupid for forgetting, and for leaving my stupid keys! Have you ever heard of 'mommy brain'? It's real, let me tell you."

"Is that when you, like, can't remember things—?"

"Can't think straight."

"Can't figure out where you parked your car."

"Can't add up a column of numbers."

"Yeah, my wife had that. We have two kids." He cast a nervous glance at Bea. "Is she okay?"

"Her eyes look really red. I could just kick myself! Could you hurry, please?"

The locksmith turned the knob and pushed open the door. Once inside, he looked around, taking in the room. He frowned. Silently asking her forgiveness, I gave Beatrice a pinch.

As her scream turned to sobs, I said over the noise, "I really appreciate it. Let me just grab my checkbook and you can get on with your afternoon." I turned away to face a cluttered table and stealthily fished a checkbook out of Bea's pouch. They were replacement checks from the local branch and had no name pre-printed on them. "How much do I owe you?" He told me, and I signed with an elaborate scrawl. "Here you go!"

"Thanks, Mrs. Brown," he said to me, taking the check. "I hope your daughter feels better." Eager to escape the near-blind baby's cries, he left.

"I'm sorry, Bunchy. I'm so sorry." After the door shut, my eyes filled with tears. I was just doing what I had to do.

As I patted her back, trying to get her to calm down, I looked around.

Something had gone very wrong here. It was still going wrong. I was in Tabitha's living room, but I was also in a dark gulley at midnight, surrounded by fallen forms hidden in shadow. The air seemed to shimmer like some weird medium resembling air. The cold was not quite real cold. Blankets lay draped over the chairs, a tray of dirty glasses on the ottoman. The rolltop desk was emptied of its drawers, its surface covered with papers and unopened mail. The stale air thrummed with unreality. Tabitha's things had become props, as in a stage set behind which nothing existed but an ink-black expanse. The room was a dead zone, a room-shaped void, hastily papered over.

Even the locksmith had sensed it, so I had to get him out quickly. Even Beatrice sensed it, and she, who normally never cried, wouldn't stop.

I saw that the bedroom door was ajar.

Hoisting the baby on my hip, I took a step in its direction, then another. I should have had someone here with me. What was I thinking, coming here alone?

With one fingertip, I pushed the bedroom door open wider. Inside, I discovered a dim space filled with the smell of illness and neglect. As my eyes adjusted to the darkness, I saw the bedclothes jump in a weak, jerky motion.

"Oh no. Tabitha…"

24

Before I started reading children's books—before *Clip-Clop* and *Chugga-Chugga Choo-Choo*, before *If You Give a Moose a Muffin* and *Room on the Broom*—I read *Contingency, Irony, and Solidarity* by the American philosopher Richard Rorty. It had caused something of a stir, and at the time I had nothing more pressing to do. So, one summer I thumbed through Rorty, hoping he'd tell me something interesting about the only topic I really cared about: myself.

Rorty began by positing that "truth" was a meaningless term. Outside the structures of human language, all notions of truth and falsehood were irrelevant and even nonsensical. He himself was not making an "argument" in an attempt to get at "truth," but simply throwing ideas out there in a stimulating way.

Rorty wrote that each person holds a set of beliefs they choose to accept as truth, and this comprises their "final vocabulary." The book's main character was a figure called "the ironist," who happened to be female in the abstract. The ironist possesses three key qualities:

(1) She has radical and continuing doubts about the final vocabulary she uses, because she has been impressed by other vocabularies, vocabularies taken as final by people or books she has encountered;

(2) she realizes that arguments phrased in her present vocabulary can neither underwrite nor dissolve these doubts;

(3) insofar as she philosophizes about her situation, she does not think that her vocabulary is closer to reality than others, that it is in touch with a power not herself.

All of this had rung true—or "true"—to me. By that point, I had read a lot of books but felt that I knew very little. I had radical and continuing doubts that anyone had ever, really, given me any useful information. The world seemed like a game of telephone in which half-truths were passed on and distorted, taking new and ever-more-dubious forms. I didn't like being an ironist, particularly; the term seemed to lock in a mood of depressive pointlessness, forever. Now here was Rorty telling me that Friedrich Nietzsche was also an ironist, as if that were a club I'd be honored to join. Nietzsche had always seemed off to me, like some annoying nerd who kept raising his hand, a nerd whose passionately high opinion of himself was not shared. Didn't he end up insane?

These days, I read *Cat in the Hat* and *Goodnight, Moon*. I read *Big Red Barn* and *But Not the Hippopotamus*. I read books about gentle, clever animals and kindly trees; books written by spinster aunts, grandmothers, and whimsical fathers; books that rhymed. I read the books that my own children would read to their children, my grandchildren: books that would or should live forever because, in their simple, unassuming way, they told the truth. Their audience was children no bigger than Charles, who clapped and said, "Again!"

The day Charles was born, I understood the hard limits of irony. As an attitude, as a pose, it was not going to help me now. I had entered the starkly literal, a world of pitiless cause-and-effect. A coin, a bath, a piece of popcorn could kill my child. A pillow, a curtain cord, a dresser not anchored to the wall. A careless mistake—the car seat installed wrong before the swerve, the late-night put-down on his stomach from which he failed to awake—could have shattering consequences. If I lost Charles, I could not get him back. My human condition was now outside the realm of wordplay or semantics; it was not a "vocabulary" at all. It was reality, and I had better figure it out fast.

What could I tell my eldest child, right off the bat? Charles, listen: Water is wet. Fire burns. An object hurtling toward the earth accelerates at 9.8 meters per second squared; it falls fast, and by then it's too late. Don't get into that car. Don't dive in shallow water. Don't let him do that. Don't be like her. Because I said so; trust me, Charles. Use your head. Think about how you'd feel if it were you. Some things are just wrong. You know better than that, don't you?

In contrast to the ironist was a slightly ridiculous figure: a dull person whom you would not want to be seated next to at a dinner party. According to Rorty, such people "think that human beings by nature desire to know." I could not speak for humanity at large, but this was true of my own children, whom I knew quite well. They "believe that there are, out in the world, real essences which it is our duty to discover and which are disposed to assist in their own discovery." (This language reminded me of Tim and his scientist friends.) They believe knowledge is "a relation between human beings and 'reality,' and the idea that we have a need and a duty to enter into this relation." A need and a duty? Well, it certainly helped, it seemed to me. And what, again, was the alternative? It had begun to seem slippery and confusing…

After two children, I was no longer an ironist. I still liked irony a lot, but at some point I had become what Rorty called a metaphysician. The other thing.

TABITHA WAS DELIRIOUS AND FRAIL. I DIDN'T KNOW WHAT WAS WRONG with her, but with heavy-lidded eyes, she seemed trapped in an agitated dream. When I found her, she could barely sit up in bed. She couldn't stand or walk. I didn't know what to do. Jeremy or Mark could arrive any minute and throw me out, so after thinking hard I placed two calls: one to Tim, asking him to please come home, and one to 9-1-1.

"It's going to be all right," I said to Tabitha. "We're going to get you out of here. I've called for help."

"Are you here for the cat?"

"No, I—"

"She must be here. I haven't seen her. What's her name?"

"Don't worry about the cat. Are you okay? I think you need to see a doctor, Tabitha. I've called the hospital. I hope that's all right."

"Is Mark here?"

"Not right now. Just me."

"I told him," she said quietly, her eyes closing. "I told him." There was no sound for a long time, and when she opened her eyes, they were glassy with tears. "I told him, *this isn't right.*"

"It isn't right. I'm sorry, Tabitha. I'm sorry I didn't get here sooner."

In the dim room, we were silent for several minutes: the pause or deep breath before things started to happen.

"You brought your little boy?" she murmured suddenly, sounding confused.

"No, he's at home. I brought my girl. Remember her?"

"Oh." Tabitha squinted at Bea. "She looks just like you."

She closed her eyes, and minutes later, an EMT rang my phone from downstairs. For the second time in three weeks, an ambulance idled outside our Spanish-style apartment building by the lake. Then Tim arrived, and suddenly the room was full and everyone had questions. Holding the baby on one hip, I brazenly lied to their faces. "We're good friends, and maybe a year ago, she gave me a spare key. I gave her one to my place too, in case I ever got locked out. And when I didn't hear from her for several weeks, I became worried."

Someone was taking vital signs, which weren't great. Tabitha was groggy and had been in bed a long time. As they readied her for transport, Jeremy appeared in the doorway, his mouth hanging open.

"Excuse me, what's going on here?"

"This is her *son*," I hissed to no one in particular.

"What are you doing here?"

Never in my life had I enjoyed lying more. "Your mother gave me a spare key! What is this, Jeremy? What were you thinking, keeping her—"

"All right, all right. My wife is understandably upset," Tim interjected.

"Are you and Mark out of your minds?" I snapped at Jeremy. "You don't leave someone alone all day in this condition and go rummaging through their *desk*—"

"This is none of your concern! I don't even know what you're doing!" he sputtered.

"Sir? Mr. Brown, is it? I need to ask you some questions about your mom."

Jeremy knew I didn't have a key. He gave me a hard look before turning toward the bedroom and his questioner.

"You and Mark should be ashamed of yourselves! What kind of sons—" I couldn't stop talking to his retreating back.

"Cara, let's go. I think we've done everything we can do here," Tim said quietly.

"Jeremy, is that you?" came a quavering, distraught voice.

"Yes, Mother! I'm coming..."

THE FINAL CALL I PLACED THAT DAY WAS TO AN ELDER ABUSE HOTLINE, and eventually the whole story came out. Tabitha's surgery had been a disaster. She had not fully understood how complicated the procedure was, and the aftermath had been terribly painful. Back at her apartment, she'd had a bad reaction to the post-surgical painkiller—nausea, vomiting, dehydration—and the experience had placed undue stress on her heart and kidneys. By the third day she was weak and disoriented, still in severe pain and unable to bear weight on her right foot. Jeremy visited her around his work schedule but was uncertain what to do. He called Mark, who was between jobs and didn't have much going on.

At some point, Mark, who was back in the States after the breakup of his marriage, found a list of passwords in Tabitha's spidery handwriting and realized he could access her bank accounts. In an experimental mood, he transferred hundreds into his name and later, growing bolder, tens of thousands. Jeremy, the diffident younger brother, went along. It was a last-ditch rebellion against the smallness of his life, its self-evident insignificance as he hit middle age, a solitary office worker barely scraping by in the city. He went along because he felt he deserved better, because he resented his wealthy mother, who still lingered on after a full life, and her oppressive cheer. After a social worker investigated, Tabitha listened carefully to her report but declined to press charges. Most of the money had gone to Mark's debts, never to be recovered, but there remained a tidy sum in Jeremy's savings, waiting for some life-changing day that never came. He offered to pay it back, but Tabitha looked away and waved him off: Don't bother.

In a meticulous address book, Tim found the names of her old friends from the dance studio and some new ones from a Tai Chi class—at eighty-two, Tabitha was not one to sit around the house—

and soon she had a parade of visitors and helpers. In her first weeks back from the hospital, I checked on her during the day and, in the evenings, when I felt newly motivated to cook, I often left the kids with Tim and took her dinner. We didn't talk about her two sons or the past. We talked about the day, the kids, the future.

And then one summer afternoon, I got a call. It was a child's voice, a girl of about nine, or maybe a young boy. "Miss Nielsen?" the voice said shyly.

"Yes?"

"I think I have your cat?"

"LOOK WHO IT IS, CHARLES! REMEMBER MEW?"

"Kitty?"

"Yes, our kitty! Well, Tabitha's kitty now. Look, she remembers you! That's right, be gentle. Nice kitty. She's been on quite an adventure, but she's home now."

"My kitty?"

"No, she belongs with Tabitha. That's her new home. But don't worry, we'll come and visit her! We'll come back and visit them both, after we move."

WHERE WERE WE GOING, WITH WHAT JOBS? WE HAD NO PLAN.

At some early point in the process of acquiring a new life, I called Ben from my old job and asked if maybe I could have it back.

"I'm sorry," I said after a pause in which my throat closed up. So, this was me: not the infamous woman who cried at work, but the woman who cried when even talking about work. "I guess Charles should go to nursery school, but Bea is just…"

"It's okay. Take your time," said Ben.

"She's still a baby. She never leaves my side all day."

"I know. I completely understand." His wife stayed home with their girls because they had money. He sounded genuinely sorry that we didn't. "You're always welcome here, Cara. Just let me know, and we'll figure out something."

"Okay. Thanks, Ben."

This brief call fortified me in some way. There were good people out there in the world. Maybe I just didn't know enough parents. I had been stuck in this stupid building, where no one remembered or knew what having little kids was like. The one exception was the Missionaries—a self-contained clan that, compared to us, seemed off-puttingly perfect.

As the weeks passed, it dawned on me that I couldn't go back to anything, certainly not my old, ho-hum job off the subway line. This was my chance to move the ball, and I could only advance forward, into the unknown. So, one night while Tim slept, I began researching points north: out of the city, past the suburbs, where the highway wound through low hills and you could finally see to the horizon. The cows would be my sign; when we saw cows, we'd be as good as home. Horses would also be acceptable, nodding at us with their big, different-shaped heads: Welcome!

In the end, it came down to a simple quid pro quo. I'd put the kids in day care and go back to work—I understood, finally, that I'd need to work—but I was not going to do it in the city. Tim wanted to look for another job here, and I wanted to stay home with the kids, but neither of us was going to get what we wanted. A terse compromise was the best we could do. After the discussion concluded, we practically shook hands. It didn't feel like marriage, really, but it felt like progress, or evolution.

It was all going to be okay. I'd been a journalist, a copy editor. It wasn't like I was going to be breaking rocks. I'd find something, and we would manage to be apart, me and the kids, until I could come get them each day. We could do this. We had to do it.

Come to think of it, I had been good at my jobs.

AND SUDDENLY IT WAS TWO MONTHS LATER, A GOLDEN FALL WITH A bite in the air. Leaves swirled around the double stroller, and as I pushed it up the hill, my back and legs felt strong. I'd done it so many times, I'd barely noticed the route getting easier.

Up in 3C, the rooms were full of moving boxes. Five years of our lives were being hastily dismantled: dishes, clothes, photo albums, stuffed animals, and dog-eared books. Without curtains, the picture windows gaped openly at the city: past the lake, over the rooftops, to distant hills covered in buildings; a vast, complex world that defied full understanding. There was no answer to the riddle of the city, and after taking it all in, I turned away.

Evil existed. A two-word lesson I could feel in my own body. It took convenient forms—despair, indifference, cruelty—whatever was at hand. It was not semantic or even situational, but real. For the first two years of my children's lives, the city was the text I read closely, attentive to any clue about how to proceed. And, hypersensitized to threat, alert to anything that might befall my children, I came to see other mothers' children clearly for the first time.

Evil was real, and I could sometimes perceive it like a shadow cast across a sunlit path. But it was not the only thing, or—ultimately—anything at all. My children's faces were infinitely more real; their peals of laughter contained more truth than the foulest depravities. As their mother, I had an ability to sense the city's traps, enticing pockets of nothingness into which the unwary tumbled. But I could also apprehend the goodness glinting everywhere, coating the world like fine gold dust, if only we could see it.

One afternoon, as I wrapped glasses in newspaper in the galley kitchen, Charles toddled up and with great effort enunciated, "Mom, may I have a cookie, please?"

"Very nice manners, Charles," I said approvingly. "Yes, you may."

ON MOVING DAY, I WAS THE LAST ONE OUT, BRINGING DOWN COATS while Tim loaded the kids into the car. Outside the elevator, I paused on the lobby's espresso-dark tile and gazed up at the distant ceiling, with its beautiful squares of gold-framed color. Already, the building in which I stood was transforming itself into a story, its cast of characters indelible in my mind forever: the Aesthete, the Old Woman, the Angry Ballerina, the Mother and Middle-Aged Daughter, the Man Downstairs.

And who were we? Who had the Nielsens been all along? The Crazy Lady and her Husband, the Bickering Couple, the Ironists, the

Noisy Family? I wasn't sure what the city thought of me, but I had an idea. Since I became a mother, it considered me unwell, paranoid, and depressed. It diagnosed me with a medical condition. It wanted me on psychotropic drugs, when often I was simply lonely. It regarded me as difficult and even hysterical; it assumed my postpartum mind was dull and days home with my children were making it duller.

But the city was wrong. For the last two-and-a-half years, I had not discerned less than other people did, but more. Because of the changes in my body, I had access to a rare and bladelike sliver of reality. I had known about Tabitha, insisted that something was wrong, when nobody had any reason to believe me. I had been right, neurologically primed to perceive and protect. I was no saint, not by a long shot—only sleep-deprived, keyed up, and biochemically optimized to see what others didn't. I'd been permitted to glimpse briefly through the scrim of this world, beyond the ordinary two-step of cause-and-effect. Though my reason remained intact, I had been privy to another kind of knowledge: numinous, mystical.

In a dim room of polished wood and colored light, I'd seen the floating woman one more time. Her face was paler than before, her features more conventionally pretty. I'd entered the old Spanish-style building on a whim because its beauty suggested an oasis of sanity. As my eyes adjusted, I saw her up at the front, as if she had been waiting for me to arrive. This time, her husband stood nearby, and she'd obviously handed him the baby—a big six-monther, rosy and fine-featured—because she had to do one thing, and it would only take a minute. Her bare white foot peeked out from under a long dress, crushing a snake.

Tears of recognition sprang to my eyes. But I also found myself laughing because I felt I knew her personally: knew all about her long, strange days, etched in eternity and somehow never-ending. She was both an icon and ordinary woman, remote in time and space, yet close as my own breath. In one effortless leap, my imagination breached the gap between us, as if that's what it had been made for all along. It seemed so normal, bearing down on a vicious snake with your bare foot while planning dinner or folding clothes or feeling your child's curious eyes on you. She was multitasking.

From outside the lobby door came two short honks. Tim had the kids strapped in, it seemed, and I was the only one missing. After one last look around, I crossed the lobby, swung open the heavy metal door, and emerged into the white-gold morning light.

With a cheery slam of the car door, I regarded my family from the shotgun seat. Tim, in a baseball cap and sunglasses, looked like a college kid embarking on a road trip. He hadn't shaved in a few days and the look suited him, I thought. In the backseat, Charles wore an airplane T-shirt and blue cotton pants. In pale pink, Beatrice serenely chewed a set of plastic keys. Both were strapped into the giant chairs we'd bought them, their own mobile thrones.

"Are you two ready for an adventure?" I asked in a lilting voice. "Are you ready to blow this town?"

Beatrice blinked at me. Charles gazed out the window and dreamily adjusted the pacifier in his mouth.

I turned back around to face Tim and said, "Let's go."

25

DURING THAT LAST YEAR IN 3C, THE THREE OF US WERE OFTEN ALONE, but we were never *really* alone. When Tim was gone, there was another male presence in 3C, one we knew well and regarded with deep affection. That fourth person was Willie Nelson. Countless afternoons, it was just me, the kids, and his two-disc compendium whose song titles—"Night Life," "Hello Walls," "Crazy," "Faded Love," and "I Gotta Get Drunk"—spoke to me, Cara Nielsen, as if reading my palm. Charles boogied around the faded rug while I waltzed with the baby. We loved all Willie's songs, but our favorite was an upbeat Western swing number recorded live with Nelson's band called "Stay A Little Longer."

In my mind's eye, I see Charles doing his stomping dance, or both children on my lap in the plush rocking chair that had soaked up every known bodily fluid. "That's a piano," I'd say, and Charles would listen, his head cocked.

"That's a guitar," I'd say.

"Kickaw."

I remember those magical days when Beatrice woke up on my pillow with a smile every morning. When Charles stopped to play in every pile of leaves, when a flight of stairs at a city park delighted him for thirty minutes. I can hardly believe that Bea was once so small, I could press her feet against my eyelids, their soles as cool and refreshing as something dreamed up in a spa, and make her laugh uproariously by peeking over them and saying *boo*.

Looking back now, I realize we were dancing to our own theme song, our own anthem, all those long, sunlit afternoons in 3C.

Stay a little longer.

IN THE STATE CAPITAL, COMMUTING DISTANCE FROM OUR TOWN, TIM IS the science advisor to a congresswoman. He can sometimes be seen explicating her positions on the evening news, and he enjoys a good relationship with local media. As a father, he is as involved as he can be, given his schedule. Along with coaching Beatrice's softball team and playing chess with Charles, he volunteers in their science classes, chaperoning field trips to planetariums, natural history museums, and robotics firms.

Gemma married Vivek in a blowout Indian ceremony, a destination wedding I did not attend. Two years later, they had twin boys: one neurotypical, the other not. These days, she's active on social media, a tireless advocate for acceptance and compassion. With all her energy and using every tool at her disposal, Gemma demands that the world make room for her boy and treat him well. If you diss him or people like him, Gemma will be happy to personally murder you. I "like" her posts, and I actually like them very much.

I may never see her again, but I feel proud of her.

Katherine Fletcher, known informally as Kit or Flee, is the artist-in-residence at a Benedictine college at the edge of a golden, undulating prairie in the Midwest. I'm curious about her work, but she has no Internet presence. Perhaps I'll visit her one day. I hope the pink scars on her wrists have healed to mere glimmers of shadow beneath the skin.

A few years back, Tabitha passed away. After the move, we spoke perhaps a dozen times before settling into an exchange of Christmas cards. One day, the executor of her estate—not Mark or Jeremy—wrote to inform me that she had left Charles and Bea generous gifts "to help with their college educations." This was so kind and so very Tabitha.

Her bequest to me came in a box in the mail: the tea set I'd admired long ago. I bought a wooden display case and stacked the delicate cups on its shelves, a reminder of what I had to work with: Sunday. Monday. Tuesday. Wednesday. Thursday. Friday. Saturday.

I WORK AT A SMALL COLLEGE DOWN THE ROAD FROM THE KIDS' SCHOOL, editing the magazine of its performing arts department. Many afternoons, like today, I work at home. I enjoy my interviews with burgeoning musicians, actors, and dancers: the artists who are always bringing us the human news.

Overall, it's a good life (and as I age, I find I'm more grateful, less inclined to complain). But it's not quite a happy ending. Our move to a commuter suburb, with a quaint Main Street and lots of children playing in front yards, made our lives easier and nicer, but it couldn't solve all our problems. After the novelty wore off, we both fell back into old ways: Tim spent long hours at the office while I toggled between the kids, housework, and work, feeling abandoned and misunderstood. We were always shouting past one another, like people separated by a crevasse, half our words dissolving into meaningless noise. Tim's mental world—my old world—now struck me as narrow and untrustworthy, full of error, while Tim bristled at the opinionated stranger in his house. We struggled to see eye-to-eye about fundamental truths, and over time, evidence piled up that I couldn't ignore: Tim had made a mistake; he'd married the wrong girl, the unconventional one who couldn't or wouldn't swim with the stream.

These days, we all hobble along, not quite a family anymore, but a family with an asterisk: a "modern" family. Occasionally at campus events, I'll run into Erin, who works in fundraising and, in her sleek blonde bob, always looks ready to shake down some millionaire. We smile and chat about the kids—this one's violin practice, that one's picky eating. She is a fun and caring stepmother, bringing certain talents to the table that I lack: baking with fondant, for example. She and Tim taught the kids to snowboard and to make pasta from scratch.

Years as a single mother strengthened me, or perhaps acquainted me with my own strength. Like Mew, I was tougher than I looked. When I first clapped eyes on James, he was doing the most uncool thing: singing in a choir. A stocky baritone with dark, curly hair and a beard, he looked to me like a medieval peasant who had just come in from a potato field to sing the "Laudate Dominum" and drink a stein of beer. I felt the sudden urge to rest my head on his shoulder and, eventually, I did.

At our wedding, Claudia said, "Well, good luck on this new… adventure." She had not quite forgiven me for leaving Tim, but I knew James would win her over. Anyway, a new adventure sounded grand.

"Thanks, Mom," I said, before being whisked off to dance with Charles, who was looking very dapper in his suit and tie.

By then, I had finally arrived in the one place where I was not weird, the place that took all of my visions and imaginings in stride. A palace of the metaphysical, it was conversant in a language I barely knew. What had seemed to me a howling wilderness was well-mapped territory after all. Someone once wrote that every modern person had to take a side: Augustine or Nietzsche, *deus* or *nihil*, love or its defining absence. After my children were born, I knew *nothing* was not the final word, though its gravitational pull was real, vertigo-inducing, and not to be underestimated. The saints had understood all this and not been frightened, but calmly and even cheerfully maintained that *all will be well…*

Whatever else it was or had been, to me the Church was distinctly maternal in spirit: the mother to whom everything matters, who weeps over every senseless cruelty—"a religion of universal anguish" per Baudelaire, who went back to it in the end. It was the mother as artist, filling the world with the iconic image of love: a young woman holding a baby on her lap. It was, for better or worse, where I belonged.

Six months after we moved, I asked my doctor to taper down my antidepressants until, eventually, I didn't need them at all. My visions subsided, and after Bea turned two, I never had another. Maybe my hormonal postpartum brain finally settled down, or maybe life just became easier without the city to contend with, and I was no longer mentally on high alert.

Occasionally I can still sense a presence not quite of-this-world, but it is gentle, vaguely boyish, and seems to enjoy watching the kids take turns pushing a merry-go-round or collapse laughing on the grass over some private sibling joke.

Each time this happens, I think of David, who never had the chance to be a child. It's funny how things turn out, because if I'd never been seated next to those two children years ago, I probably wouldn't have had kids of my own. It wouldn't have seemed important. Instead, owing to that one incident, our family has what it should have had long ago: a brother and sister growing up together with a happy, unshattered mother looking on.

So, whenever I feel that presence, I just silently tell it *thank you*, and it fades away.

CHARLES AND BEATRICE NOW HAVE TWO SETS OF PARENTS, DIFFERENT in priorities and outlook. I've always perceived more darkness than Tim has, and that's part of it. And yet at our house, we laugh all the time; there is a lot of joy spiked through this broken world. When the kids are with James and me, we regularly take them to church. Tim views this as deeply eccentric. Eventually, we'll have to discuss getting them baptized, which, given our joint custody, will be a legal as well as spiritual matter. As I understand it, the court will likely leave it up to the children when they're older, so that the choice is ultimately theirs. I have to pray and trust that both of them will find their way, in time.

They are always coming and going, modern kids with busy lives: my sensitive, intelligent Charles; my strong-willed, capable Beatrice. In my mind's eye, when I peer into the future, I see a young man who aspires to be a saint, a girl who could lead a rag-tag army to victory. Yet they are ordinary children and often misbehave.

"Please settle down!" I hiss at Mass as they goad and poke each other, giggling. "Be quiet and try to listen."

When Tim and I see each other at softball games and school recitals, we act like friendly acquaintances from way back. But there remains between us an unspoken sadness. For as long as they can remember, the kids have shuffled back-and-forth: Mom's house, Dad's house. Birthdays, holidays, summer vacations: all split up, an endless calendar of trade-offs and compromises. Their whole world is broken in half and their erring parents re-paired, while the condition of their family can never be repaired. We've failed to give them the beginning they deserve, yet I dare hope the crooked lines of their childhoods will turn out straight.

I can see by the clock that school is out. Any minute, Charles and Bea will burst through the front door. Talking and laughing, they'll make their way straight to the dining room that doubles as my office. They'll shrug their backpacks off as I greet them with hugs and ask about their day: a shining, ordinary moment in which everything will glitter like a jewel. How many such moments have I missed because the kids are at their Dad's? How many has he missed? Whatever else we gained, a treasure beyond counting slipped away.

I ask myself over and over if things could have turned out differently: if we both weren't so self-absorbed back then, if we both weren't so young. If just one person had somehow come to our aid, could we have all pulled through?

Then I recall Saint Augustine—that wayward son of a determined mother—who counsels us to entrust the past to the mercy of God.